William Leighton

The poems of William Leighton

William Leighton

The poems of William Leighton

ISBN/EAN: 9783744722933

Printed in Europe, USA, Canada, Australia, Japan

Cover: Foto ©Andreas Hilbeck / pixelio.de

More available books at **www.hansebooks.com**

THE POEMS

OF

WILLIAM LEIGHTON.

' Gone in the bloom of youth, the flower of life,
Ere yet his morning hours had wholly shone :
Gone from a world of promises how rife !
With all our bright hopes, gone !'

Complete Edition,
ILLUSTRATED BY JOHN LEIGHTON.

LONDON :
ELLIOT STOCK, 62, PATERNOSTER ROW, E.C.
1890.

PREFACE.

FORMER editions of these poems having been received with marked public favour, it is thought that a short biographical notice of the author, introducing this first complete edition, will not be considered out of place.

Descended from an old Forfarshire family, which in days gone by produced some worthy sons, William Leighton was born at Dundee on the 3rd February, 1841. His father, Mr. David Leighton—remembered for his genial manners, great intelligence and sound judgment—was the elder brother of Mr. Robert Leighton, author of 'Records, and other Poems,' which met with wide appreciation in this country, and elicited the following (among other) commendatory notices from distinguished authorities across the sea. The poet Longfellow, writing on the 15th February, 1871, said :

'I read in the papers with much pain the death of Robert Leighton, of the power and beauty of whose poems I have already expressed to you my opinion. It has not changed.'

And Ralph Waldo Emerson, on the 26th of the same month, wrote that he admired the purity and manliness of Robert Leighton's thought, and the deeply moral tone which dictated every verse, adding :

'I could not help wishing a large audience and every genial help to a poet who stooped never from the truth and dignity of his thought, and whose popularity would honour those who gave it.'

On his mother's side William Leighton was the nephew of the subject of a short biography by the late Dr. A. P. Forbes, the earnest and scholarly Bishop of Brechin, entitled 'A Memoir of the pious Life and holy Death of Helen Inglis,' published by Masters in 1854. In this memoir it is stated that Miss Inglis 'used that same happy power of insensible influence which always distinguished her, in forming the dispositions of her nephews,' and, no doubt, William Leighton in his early childhood fell under her gentle sway.

It was chiefly, however, to an excellent mother that he was indebted for the home-training that opened his mind to elevated thoughts, and contributed greatly to the formation of the pure, thoughtful and amiable character so unconsciously but clearly revealed in his writings. A devoted wife and mother, and an earnest Christian woman, Mrs. Leighton closely superintended the education of her children, besides imparting to them religious instruction and Scriptural knowledge. Having, moreover, a great taste for, and a wide acquaintance with, high-class poetical literature, she took a delight in repeating to her young people the ballads, poems, and stories which a remarkable memory and an industrious course of reading had made her familiar with. At a very early age her eldest son, William, began to show a great interest in and aptitude for learning the verses thus repeated to him, and even as an infant he was able to say very correctly, but with 'the burr of Walter Scott' (which never quite left him), many little poems and hymns to appreciative friends. A letter written by one of these to Mrs. Leighton, before William had completed his second year, refers to this accomplishment, and adds : 'That's right, Elizabeth! encourage little Willie in his love for poetry, and who knows but that he may himself become a poet.'

Mrs. Leighton continued what was to her a labour of love, and, at an age when other boys would be commencing their education, her eldest son could recite with feeling the twenty-third Psalm, the second Paraphrase, and such pieces as 'The Graves of a Household,' 'We are Seven,' 'The Loss of the Royal George,' 'The Inchcape Rock,' 'Sound the Loud Timbrel,' 'The Destruction of Sennacherib,' 'The Hymn of the Hebrew Maiden,' etc. Traces of the impressions awakened by some of these poems are noticeable, here and there, in the pieces which afterwards proceeded from his own pen; for to them Scott's words could be truly applied—

> 'And feelings, roused in life's first day,
> Glow in the line, and prompt the lay.'

The taste so early formed for committing poems to memory never left him, and year after year he added to his stock of recitals, which by-and-by included many of Longfellow's and Tennyson's choicest pieces, and other gems of modern poetry.

In his seventh year William Leighton had migrated with the family to Liverpool, where the remainder of his life was spent. At the age of nine he began to attend a day-school near Prince's Park, founded by Mr. and Mrs. John Cropper, of the Dingle, where, though the education was, technically, of a plain and limited character, the best interests of the children were studied, and life made very bright to them. Singing formed a prominent feature; the ordinary routine of school-work was relieved by the reading of interesting books; and in fine weather there were frequent excursions to the Dingle, where William, as one of the most promising scholars and chief prize-winners, received special marks of attention and favour from the kind host and hostess, for whom he always had a profound admiration.

This lovely place, where, it will be remembered, Matthew Arnold spent the last few days of his life, was then one of the prettiest spots in the neighbourhood of Liverpool. Sufficiently removed from the city's hum, these undulating grounds, ornamented with fine trees and shrubs, and running down to the water's edge, where rocky coves received the occasionally rough tides of the Mersey, left little to be desired in the way of scenery; and here, it is certain, William Leighton, in 'Summers Long Ago,' derived impressions of Nature's beauties which distinctly influenced his writings in after-years.

At an early age he entered the office of a Spanish merchant, where he remained over eight years, acquiring an intimate acquaintance with the Spanish language, and gaining the goodwill and affection of his employer and fellow-clerks. He only left this house in 1864 to accept a more promising appointment in the office of an eminent shipping firm engaged in the Brazilian trade, for whom he soon became chief and confidential clerk, and with whom he remained until his death.

Those who were associated with William Leighton in business will ever retain an appreciative recollection of his quiet, gentle manners and obliging disposition; of his clear, concise and graceful correspondence; and of his conscientious fulfilment of his duties. He was himself accustomed to say that business was a glorious institution, and that he always felt supremely happy at his work.

To return to his home life. From first to last—for William Leighton was never married—his mother was his chief adviser, confidante and friend, while she was always the object of his solicitude and affectionate care. She guided him in his lessons, and, when school-days were over, directed him in his choice of books, conversed with him about them, and took an eager, sympathetic interest in all he did. The works of all the standard poets were from time to time read and re-read, and the beautiful passages and pieces in them dwelt upon. Shakespeare was studied, and William Leighton became so well versed in the great plays, that he could tell from which of them almost any quotation, however obscure, was made. Then Longfellow's poems exercised a charm over him only to be surpassed at a later period by those of the Poet-laureate—the issue of any new volume by Tennyson filling him with enthusiasm and delight. Lesser-known poets were not neglected—Dr. Charles Mackay and Gerald Massey being favourites among these—and altogether William Leighton kept himself conversant with the poetic effusions of the day.

It became the custom to have regular literary evenings in the family circle, which was a particularly happy one, and also at the pleasant house of his uncle Robert, where kindred spirits often assembled, and he was always ready to repeat any new poem he had become acquainted with, or to enter into friendly animated discussion on the literary topics of the day. At these meetings it is remembered that some of his uncle's well-known Scottish recitations first saw the light. William wrote scarcely at all in the Doric, but he was very fond and proud of his native country, her history and scenery, and took great delight in spending his summer holidays in 'the land of mountain and of flood.'

About this time he joined several literary and debating societies, and taking an active part in their proceedings, soon became, as many of the other members delight to recollect, a fluent and effective speaker, and a favourite essay-writer; his papers on such subjects as 'Work,' 'Superstition,' 'Our Modern Minstrelsy,' etc., exciting much interest. Arising out of one of these societies a monthly manuscript magazine was started, of which he became editor, and to which he contributed both prose and verse.

His first attempts at rhyme were made before he left school, and at fifteen he began copying his verses into a book, from which many of the 'early poems' in the present collection have been transcribed. Some of his pieces he sent to a local literary paper, called *The Compass*, and others, bearing upon public events, in which he took a lively interest, were published in the *Liverpool Mercury*—all appearing either anonymously or with merely the initials 'W. L.' appended. One poem, 'The Leaf of Woodruff,' he finished with great care, and sent to the *Cornhill*, then a powerful monthly magazine under the editorship of Thackeray ; but not getting a reply for some months, he sent it to *The Compass*, and when, a few days after its insertion therein, a letter came from the *Cornhill*, accepting the poem, and enclosing a proof for revision, the young unknown author replied that it had appeared in another paper. He thus missed a chance that might have altered the tenor of his life.

As time went on his duties and responsibilities increased, and with curtailed leisure he could write pieces but occasionally, and these were shown to only a few select friends. Indeed, he attached but slight importance to his own productions, and would never repeat them in the home circle, or at penny readings, which he took a delight in assisting to promote for the entertainment of the working-classes at Bootle, where the family then resided, and at which he became popular as a reader and reciter, excelling in such pieces as 'The Soldier of the Legion,' 'The Lord of Burleigh,' 'The May Queen,' 'Somebody's Darling,' etc.

Very few, therefore, save his intimate friends, knew that he had any poetical gift. Those who did know urged on him the advisability of publishing his poems, and at length, yielding to their persuasions, he began writing them out for that purpose, and had made considerable progress with his task, just reaching that part of 'The Lovers' where the hero is described as being attacked by fever, when he was himself suddenly stricken down with typhoid fever, which in ten days proved fatal. He passed away as the sun was setting on the evening of the 22nd April, 1869, at the early age of twenty-eight, to the inexpressible grief of his relatives and friends, to whom he had endeared himself by his sweet disposition and exemplary character, and by whom fond hopes had been cherished as to the position he might afterwards attain among the poets of the day.

His remains were interred in Anfield Cemetery, his friend, Dr. W. M. Taylor, now of New York, conducting the ceremony, and a verse of his own was inscribed on the tombstone :

> ' Mourn not this earth with its languishing bloom ;
> Grieve not to go from its darkness and strife ;
> Beauty is brighter beyond the tomb,
> And death alone leads to perfect life.'

A stained-glass window, ' In loving memory of William Leighton,' and illustrating two of his poems—' The Night Cometh,' and ' Peace, be still '—has since been placed in the pretty church of St. Anne's, Brookfield, Highgate Rise, in the north-west of London.

In the year 1870 a large collection of his pieces, entitled ' Poems by the late William Leighton,' was published, and met with a very favourable reception, soon passing into a second edition. Smaller publications of selected pieces subsequently appeared, and received a full meed of popular favour, one of them, ' Baby Died To-day, and other Poems,' obtaining a wide circulation.

These being all out of print, and continual inquiries being made for the poems, the present complete edition is now issued, containing many pieces never before published, together with a portrait of the author, and ten illustrations by Mr. John Leighton, a son of the author of 'Records.'

The poems have been arranged as nearly as possible in their chronological order,

> ' As they came—the latest last,
> That he who deigns to listen to their chimes
> May tell how wore the heart from which they passed.'

The productions of his boyhood appear first, then the pieces composed while he was a comparatively irresponsible clerk, and finally the poems written during his last years in the intervals of busy commercial life. A melancholy interest attaches to the latest piece of all—' At Death's Door '—it having been pencilled by him during the first few days of his fatal illness. It was his first serious ailment, for up to that time he had enjoyed excellent health, and yet he seemed instinctively to know that his end was drawing near, and to re-echo the sad refrain in which he had foreshadowed the early closing of his life's short day :

> ' And now the night stolen on me like a thief,
> While yet I dreamt that it was scarcely noon ;—
> Sad that the sunshine is so very brief !
> Sad that the shadows fall so very soon !'

Those who may be interested in this imperfect sketch will be gratified to know that William Leighton's good mother still survives, beloved and respected by a large circle of relatives and friends, and exercising her gentle, elevating influence over the children of another generation.

January, 1890.

CONTENTS.

EARLY POEMS: 1856—1861.

Contents.

POEMS: 1862—1865.

Contents. XV

Contents.

EARLY POEMS.

1856—1861.

INTRODUCTORY STANZAS.

Come, Poesie, thou well-belovèd thing,
  And make thy home in this wild-beating heart ;
Come, tune my tongue, and make me fit to sing
  Thy praises : bright and beautiful thou art !

Come, Poesie, thou fountain of delight,
  And bathe my soul in thy pellucid stream ;
Come, glide into my being, pure and bright ;
  Come, visit me like a delightful dream !

Sweet Poesie, I've seen thee in the day,
  And in my dreams by night I've heard thy voice
Speaking unto my soul : thou seemed'st to say,
  'Come with me ; I will make thy heart rejoice !'

Sweet Poesie, oh, were it not for thee
  My life would be a weary life of care,
And this bright world so beautiful to see
  A dreary desert full of dark despair.

I—2

Wild Poesie, put in my hands a lyre,
  That, when I sweep my fingers o'er its chords,
My heart may catch some of thine own wild fire,
  And breathe it forth in all my works and words!

Wild Poesie, oh, may I hear thy voice
  In the sweet rustling of the forest trees;
Oh, may I hear it in the ocean's noise;
  Oh, may I hear it in the whispering breeze!

Dear Poesie, I'll wear thee near my heart;
  Thou art a pearl of greatest price to me:
If thou wilt stay with me my better part
  Of life I'll gladly dedicate to thee!

Dear Poesie, bright like the morning come,
  And sun my soul in radiance divine:
Come, make within this throbbing heart a home!
  Come, I would worship at thy hallowed shrine!

SUMMERS LONG AGO.

How sweet to me the memories of happy days of
    youth,
When my heart was full of gladness and my smile
    was full of truth;
When everything I gazed upon seemed beautiful
    and fair,
And all the livelong summer day I never knew a
    care;
When I could scarcely understand such things as
    grief and woe;—
Ah! those were happy, happy days,—those
    summers long ago!

The merry birds sang joyously, the sun shone
    brighter then,
The flow'rets grew more fragrantly down in the
    grassy glen,

The waters had a brighter flash, and bluer was the
    sky,
And greener were the forest trees that waved
    their branches high,
And sweeter was the gentle breeze that thrilled a
    music low
Throughout my heart, and made me love those
    summers long ago.

Then, stretched beneath the forest trees, upon the
    ground I lay,
And heard the rustling of their leaves through the
    long summer day;
The happy carol of the thrush, the blackbird's
    whistle clear,
Like softly whispered melodies fell gently on my
    ear,
And like Æolian harpings sweet the prattling
    brooklet's flow
Gushing and bright came o'er my heart in summers
    long ago.

And when the sun with fiery face was sinking fast
    to rest,
And evening's dim pale glimmering star was
    twinkling in the west,

Oh, how I loved to wander then at twilight's
    dreamy hour,
To feel the freshness of the breeze, the fragrance
    of the flower,—
To gaze in transport at the heavens, and wonder
    at the glow—
The purpling glow of eventide in summers long
    ago!

Ah! those indeed were happy days; my heart knew
    nought of guile,
And all God's earth then seemed to me one uni-
    versal smile!
And oft amid this stern world's strife my memory
    ponders o'er,
And fondly dwells upon those days,—those joyous
    days of yore:
The silent stars may cease to shine, and all things
    fade below,
But I never, never can forget the summers long
    ago!

'JESUS WEPT.'

(JOHN xi. 35.)

THE Man of Sorrows stood beside the tomb,
   Beneath whose shadow lay the friend He loved,
And as He gazed into its silent gloom,
   Unspoken anguish deep His spirit moved.
He gazed in pity on the mourning throng—
   Those few sad friends who weeping vigil kept,—
His loving look on Mary lingered long,
   His trembling bosom heaved, and ' Jesus wept.'

The Saviour wept ! how precious were the tears
   That streamed in sorrow from His holy eyes ;
We think of them and calm our troubled fears ;
   We think of them, and all *our* sorrow flies !
Our hearts no longer feel the sickening doubts—
   The darkling gloom that o'er the soul had
      crept—
No longer heed the cold world's haughty flouts,
   Or mark its mockery since the Saviour wept !

Thou sinner, mourning o'er thy evil ways,
    Oh, know there still is pardon offered free!
Then why not join with those who sing the praise
    Of Him who lived, who wept, who died for thee?
Thou silent mourner, sorrowful and lone,
    Weeping o'er joys that long have buried slept
In the sad tomb of Memory, weep on,
    For tears are holy things since ' Jesus wept !'

THE MAIDEN'S SONG.

'Twas evening, in the summer time,
   The breeze was low and mild,
The sun before he sank to rest
   On all glad nature smiled,
While at her little cottage door
   Lingered a lovely child.

A feverish flush was on her face,
   A glow was in her eyes,
As with a longing gaze she looked
   At the softly purpling skies,
Which to her childish fancy seemed
   The gates of Paradise.

That fell disease had marked the maid,
   That waits not the blooming prey;
But she felt the life return to her
   On that glorious summer day;
And she rose and went to the cottage door
   To see the children play.

The setting sun in glory streamed
    Upon her silvery hair;
It lit her face as if it loved
    To dwell on aught so fair,
As in a voice of sweetest tone
    She sang a simple air;—

A song to Him whose name is Love,
    To Him who reigns on high;
And Jesus' name the burden was
    Of that simple melody;
The echoes catch the gentle strain,
    As if loath to let it die.

She ceased, and the golden summer sun
    Sank in the gorgeous west,
And the lady moon appeared to view,
    In her borrowed glory drest,
As the little maiden left the door
    And slowly went to rest.

    *   *   *   *   *

'Twas midnight, and the dreamy stars
    Were twinkling overhead,
When weeping friends were gathered round
    That suffering maiden's bed,
And like the flash of an angel's wing
    Her gentle spirit fled.

Yet, ere she left this earthly scene,
     Like the sound of Seraphs' throng,
There came a strain so soft and clear
     Which the midnight airs prolong ;
And the tune that fell on the listening ear
   · Was the same as the maiden's song.

A happy smile plays o'er face ;
     She opes her closing eyes,
As the sun gleams for a moment forth
     From the darkly-clouded skies,—
But a shadow chases away the smile,
     And the little maiden dies.

*   *   *   *   *

But oft when evening settles down
     On trees and whispering fanes,
When shadows clothe the mountains brown
     And lengthen o'er the plains,
A silvery voice is heard to sing
     Those sweet and soothing strains.

Oh, who shall say she does not leave
     Her home in happier sphere,
An angel on some mission bent—
     To wipe away the tear,—
To guide to realms beyond the stars,—
     To praise her Saviour here ?

FAREWELL TO THE BARQUE.

Farewell to the barque! see how swiftly she's
    flying !
  Her prow cuts the waves as they ripple along ;
The gentle south wind through her rigging is
    sighing,
  And the sailor sings sadly his farewell song,—
He sings his farewell to the land of his birth,
  To his home, to his kindred, and all he holds
    dear,
And he thinks his own land is the best spot on
    earth,
  As down his brown cheek rolls the sorrowful
    tear.

Farewell to the barque ! see how stately she
    glides,
  With her tall, tapering spars towering up to the
    skies !

Regardless alike of the wind and the tides,
  Like a dream of the morning, on, onward she
    flies ;
With her streamers aloft and her snowy sails
    spread,
  Like a vision of beauty she gleams on our sight;
Far, far to the horizon's verge she has sped,
  And shows by the setting sun glorious and
    bright.

Farewell to the barque !   Ah, for ever farewell !
  When yon sun disappears from those soft
    purpling skies,
When the ocean waves heave with their dark
    midnight swell,
  That barque may for ever be lost to our eyes !
But o'er uncertain evils, oh! why should we mourn,
  Or foretell the tales that seem doubtful and
    dark ?
That ship in her splendour may safely return
  And gladden our hearts—then farewell to the
    barque !

OUR CHILDHOOD'S PRAYER.

We may pass through the world amid pleasure's
      beams,
And glide o'er the waves of sunshiny streams;
Or 'mong glooms and shades we may sadly rove
Without one bright sunbeam of joy or love
To gladden our hearts where'er we may roam,
Or gleam o'er our paths like a smile from home;—
But whate'er our fate be—pleasure or care—
Oh, we never forget our childhood's prayer!

Memories of youth may be lost in the past,
And its dreams may fade before sorrow's blast;
But one memory can ne'er forgotten be,—
'Tis the prayer we lisped at a parent's knee!
Other things may fade from the heart that will,
But that keeps its place on its tablet still;
For a mother's voice has imprinted there
The hallowed words of our childhood's prayer!

As a traveller far from his native shore,
Which he knows he never may look on more,
Mid joy or grief will recall to his mind
Some loved scene sadly left behind :—
So do we look back to our earlier days,
Amid sorrow's glooms or mid pleasure's rays ;
And falling like balm through the holy air
Come the simple words of our childhood's prayer!

THOU ART GONE, MY BROTHER.

Thou art gone, my brother, from earth away,
To dwell in realms of endless day;
And the night-winds sigh and the flow'rets wave
Above thy lone and silent grave :
And we miss the sound of thy merry voice
That filled the house with such sweet noise :
Thy sunny smile and thy joyous mirth
Have passed for ever from the earth.

Thou art gone, my brother, to lands above,
Where all is peace and joy and love ;
To bask in everlasting rays,
And hymn the great Eternal's praise :
Where a hand of love and pity dries
The sorrowful tears from weeping eyes ;
Where thousands round the Saviour stand,
With crowns on head and harps in hand.

Thou art gone, my brother, to climes afar,
Where seraphs, saints, and angels are :

Where fruits and flowers immortal grow,
And silent streams of silver flow ;
Where sweet sounds float on the balmy air,
Where all is pure and bright and fair :
Through the dark portals of the tomb
Thou hast passed to that land of bliss and bloom !

But although thou art gone, my brother dear,
Oh, say dost thou ever linger here ?
Dost thou leave that land of joy and bliss
To visit the scenes of thy life in this ?
Dost thou ever return to this lowlier earth,
And mix with the throng round our happy hearth?
Dost thou join in our sorrows and share our tears?
Dost thou calm our doubts and soothe our fears ?

Ah yes ! when we join our evening prayer,
Thou, bright spirit, art hovering there !
When we sing our nightly song of praise,
With a loving smile thou hear'st our lays :
And in the watches of the night
Thou art standing near with thy wings of light,
And we feel the glory that round thee beams,
And see thy face among our dreams.

And still wilt thou guide us until we stand
Upon the shores of that happy land ;

Still wilt thou watch us by night and day,
Till calmly and gently we pass away;
Then, on thy shining pinions bright,
Thou wilt bear us to realms of love and light,—
And in those regions by angels trod,
We will dwell with thee—we will dwell with God.

TOLL THE BELL.

Toll the bell, 'tis Sabbath even ;
  Let it echo through the air,
Like a voice from yon blue heaven
  Calling to the house of prayer.

Speaking gently to our hearts,
  Calmly does its cadence fall ;
Softly, softly it imparts
  Joy, and peace, and love to all !

Toll the bell, then, sweetly, slowly,
  Through the still and solemn hour ; .
Let the lofty and the lowly
  Share alike its soothing power.

Toll the bell, 'tis Sabbath even,
  And I would I could reveal
All the longings through me driven,
  All the fancies that I. feel :—

'Toll the bell, 'tis Sabbath even ;
Let it echo through the air,
Like a voice from yon blue heaven
Calling to the house of prayer.'

Longings all too deep to utter—
  Thoughts that never can be told,
Save in an imperfect mutter,
  Feeble, passionless, and cold!

Oh, my heart is well-nigh bursting
  With the thoughts I cannot speak,
And my soul is thirsting, thirsting,
  For the joys I dare not seek.

Could I, could I e'er inherit
  Pens of poets passed away,—
Could I have their brain and spirit
  Dwelling in me night and day;—

Then would I pour forth my numbers
  Through the atmosphere of Time,
Like that bell which wakes men's slumbers
  With its sweet and soothing chime!

Toll the bell, 'tis Sabbath even;
  Let it echo through the air,
Like a voice from yon blue heaven
  Calling to the house of prayer!

ELLA.

Sʜᴇ played, a bright and blue-eyed girl,
    Before her cottage door ;
Her golden hair in many a curl
    Her shoulders fair hung o'er :
From childhood's earliest days she loved
    To watch the silvery beam
Of the sweet moon, as light it moved
    Along her village stream.

She left her home a blushing bride—
    She left her village too ;—
The stately husband by her side
    Her feelings never knew :
Nor how a tear stood in her eye
    That dimmed its azure gleam :
Nor why she breathed a deep-drawn sigh
    At parting with the stream.

She went where form the gay and proud
 A world within their own ;
The centre of an envying crowd,
 She stood as one alone :
And when on every tongue her grace
 And beauty was the theme,
She longed once more the bee to chase
 Beside her native stream.

She sought a land which ever smiles
 Back to the smiling sun ;
Where odours float from balmy isles,
 And streams of silver run :
Yet ev'n mid these she longed for night,
 For then, in some sweet dream,
She stood again beside her bright
 And beauteous village stream !

Again she sought her childhood's home,
 But, ah ! how changed was she !
For Death had whispered to her, ' Come
 And make thy home with me !'
She lingered the long winter through,
 And heard the owlet's scream
Among the leafless trees that grew
 Beside her village stream.

Slow passed the dreary winter hours ;
  The soft winds came once more ;
The sun awoke the early flowers
  Before her cottage door :—
But ere the trees began to wave
  Their green leaves in his beam,
They laid her in the quiet grave
  Beside her native stream.

FRAGMENT.

How sweet, when solemn silence reigns around,
When twilight shadows lengthen o'er the ground,
To wander through the sweetly scented grove
And listen to the voice of one we love.
The nightingale pours forth among the trees
Her plaintive music on the passing breeze ;
The dreary murmur of the prattling rill
Falling upon the ear so soft and still,
The star of evening twinkling in the west—
All these beget within the lover's breast
Sweet dreams of bliss and never-ending rest.

Sweet hour of twilight, when the broad big sun
Sinks down to rest, his course of beauty run ;
When fairies glide along the silent streams,
And bathe their beauty in the pale moonbeams ;
When Poets' spirits leave the earth and rise
To scenes of glory 'mong the starry skies !

Oh, how I love to wander at that hour,.
When dews are falling on the closing flower,
With thee of beauty's crown the brightest gem,
A peerless pearl in nature's diadem ;—
To feel the unalloyed, enraptured bliss
That thrills my heart at beauty's magic kiss ;
To clasp the form that makes my soul rejoice,
Or list the strains seraphic of thy voice ;
To gaze in rapture at thy soft blue eyes,
Or scan the glorious star-bespangled skies ;
O sweetest hour for friendship or for love,
A foretaste of the joys of heaven above !

KATE.

Some covet earthly fame, some seek to gain a
    name,
  Some snatch at laurels that soon fade away ;
Some on ' proud honour's field,' grasping the
    sword and shield,
  Rear their proud crests in the midst of the fray.

Some plough the ocean old, some live to heap up
    gold,
  Some strive to manage the helm of the State ;
But my ambition is naught more or less than
    this,
  To live in the love of my beautiful Kate.

Her hair is of silvery hue, her eyes are of softest
    blue,
  Her breath is as sweet as the rose on the lea,
And like a joyous spring lovingly murmuring,
  So seems her gentle voice whispering to me.

Soft is her sunny smile, free from all taint of guile;
   Clear is her heart from all feelings of hate;
Pure as the snowy flake, smooth as the glassy
     lake,
   Is the fair bosom of beautiful Kate.

Oh, that it were our lot in some sequestered spot
   Where the sweet summer eternally stays,
Where the soft sighing gales play through the
     mystic vales,
   Calmly to live till the end of our days.

While we were blessed with health, I'd never sigh
     for wealth,
   I'd never envy the lot of the great;
In her fond loving kiss I would know perfect bliss,
   Riches I'd find in the heart of my Kate.

There at the noontide heat, on the fair arbour seat,
   Together we 'd sit and gaze into the stream,
Rolling its tide along sweet as the linnet's song,
   Bright as the hues of a young poet's dream.

No grief or worldly strife e'er should embitter life,
   No gloom or shadow on us lay its weight;
Into our happy home no cankering care should
     come;
   Nothing should sadden the heart of my Kate.

And at the dewy eve, there would we sit and
weave
Tissues as bright as the butterfly's wings,
Dreams of a world afar in the pale evening star,
Visions of love and all beautiful things.

There we'd find lasting bliss, pleasure and happi-
ness,
Nothing so dear as our own garden-gate;
Nothing so calm and still as the pure winding rill;
Nothing so sweet as the smile of my Kate.

There we'd find perfect joy, pleasures without
alloy;
There we would revel in rivers of love;
There would all turmoils cease, there would we
dwell in peace,
Tasting the joys of the ransomed above.

And when I felt the breath of the grim King of
• Death
Whisper the fast-coming end of my date,
Calmly I would repose, and at life's evening's
close
Breathe forth my soul on the bosom of Kate.

*   *   *   *   *

Softly, what do I hear falling upon my ear,
　　Like the soft voice of an angel of light—
‘ Lo, thou hast dreamed away all the long sum-
　　　　mer day ;
　　Rouse thee, and join in mortality’s fight.

‘ Join in the onward strife, strive for the upward
　　　　life ;
　　Never rebel ’gainst the mandates of Fate,—
Cherish a noble aim, struggle to gain a name ;
　　Live to be worthy the love of thy Kate.’

AN INTRODUCTION FOR AN ALBUM.

Reader, whate'er thy name may be,
  Whate'er thy station, sex, or age,
Lo! thou must pay the penalty,
  And add a trifle to my page!

Art thou a maiden young and free,
  Thy fancies teeming fresh and fair,
Leave not this book until you see
  Your own bright thoughts reflected there.

Art thou a lover, take thy pen
  And write a lay to faithful love—
The chiefest bliss of lowly men,
  The chiefest joy of saints above.

Art thou a young and bright-souled one,
  Open thy spirit and unfold
Its thoughts, that we may gaze upon
  The glory-glimpses you behold!

3

Art thou a man of troubled life,
  Speak of the time when care shall cease.
Art thou a soldier, tell of strife ;
  Art thou a poet, sing of peace.

Art thou a pilgrim old and gray,
  Toil-stained and weary of the road,
Yet heavenward bent, teach us the way
  To grasp the outstretched hand of God !

SONG.

I LOVE the blue of the violet fair,
  In the beauteous sunshine glowing,
When it sheds its perfume on the air,
  All its azure glories showing !
    But the bloom forsakes the violet's face,
    And its gaudy glory dies,
    Whene'er I fondly seek to trace
    The depth of thine azure eyes.

I love the blue of the summer sky
  When the early lark is singing,
And when the stars are twinkling high,
  And the evening bells are ringing ;
    But dim to me is the starlight's gleam,
    And the softly purpling skies,
    When compared to the brightly shining beam
    That dwells in thy soft blue eyes.

3—2

I love the blue of the mighty deep
    When the ocean waves are flying,
Or when its breast is hushed to sleep,
    And the gentle breeze is sighing ;
        But tame to me is the blue of the sea,
            The violet and the skies,
        Whene'er I fondly gaze on thee,
            And thrill beneath thine eyes.

BEAUTY.

Beauty wins all my worship : I can gaze
    Upon a scene of loveliness until
A blissful rapture through my being plays,
    And both mine eyelids fill.

Rising and setting suns possess the power
    To stir my spirit with their mystic leaven ;
And in the petals of a simple flower
    I see a glimpse of heaven.

A summer morning melts into my soul ;
    A gurgling streamlet gushes o'er my heart ;
A happy blaze of sunlight bids the whole
    Of this world's cares depart.

Whate'er in Art or Nature that excels—
    In all things pure, and holy, and refined
From outward dross of earth—there beauty dwells
    Eternally enshrined !

Its essence permeates the atmosphere ;
  To fix its form in stone the sculptor tries
And I have drunk its spirit from the clear
  Blue depths of pictured eyes.

Therefore I count its sweetness all divine,
  And my deep-drawn devotion long to prove,
The while I burn upon its sacred shrine
  The incense of my love.

Nor is this love idolatry, for in
  The lowliest flower that rises from the sod
We lose all sense of earthliness and sin,
  And stand alone with God !

And while our eyes with tears of rapture swim,
  The spirit rises on ecstatic wings,
And yearns for closer intercourse with Him
  From whom all beauty springs.

IN ABSENCE.

When morning blushes in the sky,
   And Sol begins his daily duty,
While yet the lark sings loud and high,
   And all the Orient glows in beauty,
And every flower is hung with dew
That sparkles bright, I think of you.

Through all the sultry hours of day
   I miss the music of your voice,
And nurse those memories fond and gay,
   Which make the lonely heart rejoice ;
And like a river coursing through
The soul, my thoughts flow on to you.

And when the daylight fades and dies,
   And twilight falls upon the earth,
And through the dusky evening skies
   Lone Hesper slowly glimmers forth,
I think of joys which once I knew
At that sweet dreamy hour with you.

And when the dusk is drowned in dark,
  Through all the still star-spangled night,
Until the carol of the lark
  Awakes the mist-wrapt world to light,
And morning's tearless eyes of blue
Shine sweetly down, I dream of you !

ROBERT BURNS.

(Written for the Burns Centenary, 25th January, 1859.)

AND dost thou say the peasant bard
  Who held the plough on Scotia's plains
Had scorn for good, and no regard
  For Him whose life leaps in our veins?

Weak-minded fool, dost thou not know
  The poet's heart is ever true,
And turns to God, as rivers flow
  To regions which their rising knew?

The clouds seem dark as o'er the blue
  And broad expanse of heaven they glide,
But He whose eye can pierce them through
  Sees silver on the other side.

The clouds *seem* dark, and yet they shed
  The dews and sweet refreshing showers
That make the daisy raise its head,
  And breathe a fragrance 'mong the flowers.

And so with Burns; look through his sin,
His follies, frailties, and excess,
And you will see a soul within
Whose silver side was manliness.

Yes, like the clouds, he poured the balm
Of joy o'er many a wounded heart;
The troubled breast he soothed to calm,
He made the tear of pity start.

And though the hours of darkness came,
And through that darkness he was driven,
His song—his heart—were still the same;
His destination still was heaven.

And now, tho' reached that unknown shore
From whence no mortal e'er returns,
Thousands of hearts when we're no more,
Will bless the name of Robert Burns.

GONE!

Gone are the visions of life's early morning—
  Those dreams of delight that illumined my way!
Gone! all are gone! but their memory, returning,
  Oft gleams o'er my heart like the sun's setting
    ray.

Gone are the hopes then so fondly I cherished—
  The raptures and joys of my boyhood's bright
    hours;
The madness, the mirth, and the laughter have
    perished,
  And faded away like the bloom from the flowers.

Gone are the friendships I once prized so dearly;
  The loves I once fostered have flown from my
    sight;
And the music of morning, that once sounded
    clearly,
  Has melted away in the murmur of night.

Dreams of my childhood, oh, why did ye leave
　　me?
　　Ye were so beauteous, so fresh and so fair !
Why, say, oh why did ye, flitting, deceive me ?
　　Wherefore so transiently fade into air ?

Joys, bright and blooming, oh, why have ye
　　vanished,
　　　Leaving no pure ray to gleam through the
　　　gloom ?
Hopes, rainbow-coloured, oh, why are ye banished,
　　To bloom not again on this side the tomb ?

Fate, thou stern monarch, oh, why didst thou
　　sever
　　Hearts that in love and affection entwined ?
Why didst thou breathe o'er our souls the ' for
　　ever '
　　That scattered our raptures and hopes to the
　　wind ?

Alas ! such is life ; amid silence and sorrow
　　We tread the bleak path of this cold world
　　　alone ;
We hopefully look for the joys of the morrow :
　　Ere that morrow has passed its transports have
　　　flown !

But why should we murmur ? 'Tis useless re-
    pining ;
We know the high Hand that inflicteth the rod ;
And lustrous with love we may see His face
    shining,
Though we bend 'neath the stroke of a chasten-
    ing God !

OH, SAY NOT THIS WORLD IS ALWAYS AS DARK.

Oʜ, say not this world is always as dark
   As it seems in our moments of sorrow ;
For the croak of the raven, the song of the lark,
   May ring through the heavens to-morrow.
Then why should we play the misanthrope fool,
   And sit in our dungeon of sadness,
While over the glooms of Hegesia's school
   We may fly on the free wings of gladness !

Our loves may be false and our friends turn un-
      kind,—
   For but few friends, alas ! ere prove true ones ;
Though we mourn them with grief we should still
      bear in mind
   'Tis not very hard to·get new ones !
We look on the meadows, the trees and the skies,
   'And we marvel how men can adore them ;
But we think not the jaundice is in our own eyes,
   And 'tis *that* throws the yellow tint o'er them !

And though oft we find thorns where we thought
    to have flowers,
  Why, why, should we harbour resentment ?
There is not a man in this wide world of ours
  Who has not great cause for contentment !
Then say not this world is always as dark
  As it seems in our moments of sorrow,
For the croak of the raven, the song of the lark,
  May ring through the heavens to-morrow.

SUNSET.

I WANDERED at evening beside the still sea,
  When the rays of the setting sun streamed o'er
    its breast,
And the sigh of its wavelets was wafted to me
  By the soft breeze that came from the rosy-
    heavened West.

All calmly its waters lay stretched at my feet,
  Not a ripple was seen on its surface of light,
And afar, where the soft sky and bright waters
    meet,
  The sun was descending fast, fast from my
    sight.

But even when he had sunk in his watery shroud,
  And faded away from my strained gazing eyes,
His soft light still lingered in every gay cloud,
  And the waters reflected the glow of the skies.

It seemed as if Sol, as he sank down to rest,
  Dispersed all his glories and rays at his back,
As a vessel when sailing o'er Ocean's wide breast,
  Leaves behind her the white foam that gleams
    on her track.   ·

'Tis e'en thus with the fast-fading joys of this
    world ;
  Like the sun they sink down in the waves of
    the past ;
And our heart-hopes are oft from their pinnacles
    hurled,
  And laid low in the dust by affliction's rude
    blast.

Yet, although we may stand on the brink of de-
    spair,
  When the sun of our joys is descending in
    night,
Still memory will bring back some raptures that
    were,
  As the sun leaves behind him some rays of his
    light.

INTRODUCTION,

FOR A MANUSCRIPT MAGAZINE.

As some brave ship, launched on the heaving
    main,
That carries wealth to distant unknown shores,
And laden with rich freight of precious stores,
Bounds swiftly homeward o'er the waves again :—
So do we send thee forth, in simple trust
That thou wilt safely weather every gale
Of critic harshness which may rend thy sail,
Or strain thy timbers with its angry gust.
Bring riches back to heart and mind and brain,
For which thought in the mines of knowledge
    delves;
Our truest wealth is garnered in ourselves,
And giving ever yields the greatest gain !
Oh, may each heart some golden full ear glean
From out the stubble of our Magazine !

MARIANA'S SONG.

The day is lonely, very lonely ;
  I would that it were night !
The sunshine has no charm for me,
  Though it is warm and bright ;
It only mocks my misery
  With its gaudy, glaring light !

The night is lonely, very lonely ;
  Oh, will the day dawn soon ?
The darkness brings no rest for me,
  The night denies its boon ;
And through the long lone hours I see
  Naught but the pale-faced moon.

My heart is lonely, very lonely ;
  I would that I could find
Some breast to share this misery
  That weighs so on my mind ;
Something to yield that sympathy
  Denied me by my kind.

4—2

My life is lonely, very lonely ;
　　Yet often-times I hear
Some strains of sweetest melody
　　Strike softly on mine ear ;
And I long for the time when my life will be
　　No longer lone and drear !

THE RIVER OF LIFE.

I stood beside the river,
Where beech-trees moan and shiver,
And waters roar upon the shore,
And waves roll on for ever.

Here oft the low wind sigheth,
The sea all stilly lieth,
And croaking note from sea-bird's throat
In the far distance dieth,

Yet oftentime it rageth
And every wave engageth,
And near and far a deadly war
Its boiling billow wageth!

But when in calm or motion,
With ceaseless strange devotion,
Its rolling tide doth onward glide
Toward the wailing ocean.

On, onward still it goeth,
Nor rest nor respite knoweth,
Till lulled to sleep in ocean deep,
Where the red coral groweth !

This life is like a river,
Whose waters quail and quiver;
With ceaseless flow they onward go
Toward the great ' for ever.'

Some lives glide sweetly, slowly,
Mid music soft and holy,
Like moonlight's gleam across a stream,
When wavelets ripple lowly.

While some, their crests uprearing,
Undaunted and unfearing,
Roll through the sky all wild and high,
The clouds of heaven nearing !

Here some are sighing sadly;
Here some are moaning madly ;
While now, anon, their sorrows gone,
Some eyes are gleaming gladly.

Despising, hating, loving,
Despair and rapture proving,
The power of soul linking the whole,
They still keep onward moving.

All roll on like the river,
And all their waves deliver
To Him of life the Giver,
Till in the sea, Eternity,
They sink to rest for ever!

SHE CAME—AND WENT.

She came, as comes the morning light
After a dark and troublous night ;
And hearts that long had swooned in pain,
When she appeared revived again.

She came, as comes the joyous Spring,
With light and glory on her wing,
And all who saw her bent to praise
Her beauty, loveliness, and grace.

She came, as come the beauteous flowers,
Opening unseen in summer hours,
And spread around that silent spell,
Which made all spirits love her well.

Oh, had she lingered yet awhile
To bless us with her glorious smile,
Our souls had felt the loving glow !
Our hearts had ne'er been plunged in woe !

She was a star, whose holy light
Gleamed softly through the gloomy night,
Whose beam of glory gladdens yet :—
Alas, that she so quickly set !

She was a bright and glorious dream,
All silvered o'er with beauty's beam ;
Whose memory lingers to the last :—
Alas, that she so quickly passed !

She went, as sinks the setting sun,
His bright brief course of beauty run,
When at the loveliest hour of day
He melts in his own light away.

She went, as fades some beauteous star
Set in the firmament afar,
Which, when the darkness glides away,
Is hidden in the light of day.

She went, as dies the fading rose,
When evening airs whisper repose ;
But, like the withered rose's breath,
Her fragrance lingers after death !

Ev'n in the midst of beauty's bloom
She sought the shadow of the tomb :
But had she lived—oh, who can tell
The hopes of those who loved her well !

Why did she die—so fair, so young—
The varied song of life unsung?
So bright, so pure—why did she die?
Alas! alas! we know not why!

We can but trust 'tis for the best;
She now hath found a home of rest!
One flow'ret more from earth is riven,
One flow'ret more doth bloom in heaven!

THINK NOT, ALTHOUGH I MINGLE HERE.

Think not, although I mingle here
  Among the gayest of the gay,
That memory never drops a tear
  For her, the maiden far away.
This gay demeanour only hides
  A heart that wastes with wild regret,
As deepest streams have smoothest tides—
  No, no, I never can forget.

Oft when I join the thoughtless throng
  Who still to pleasure's temples fly,
From the wild mirth of dance and song
  I turn to heave a secret sigh ;
For though I've ta'en a last adieu,
  Still must the memory linger yet
Of days when I believed her true—
  No, no, I never can forget.

WRITTEN IN MY SISTER'S ALBUM.

My sister; could an honest prayer,
　　Breathed in an Ear which ever hears,
Preserve thy future life from care,
　　And joyful make the coming years,

That　prayer　would　pierce　heaven's star-
　　arched zone
　　And beg the God of Love to bless,
Till angels standing near the Throne
　　Would wonder at its earnestness !

Yet well I know that joy and care
　　Must in each life co-mingled be :—
Would I might all thy sorrows bear,
　　And leave the joys alone to thee !

But years will come and years will go,
　　And every year will bring its share
Of joy and sorrow, bliss and woe,
　　Which all unaided thou must bear ;

And those dear eyes, that ever now
　Brim o'er with all the joys of youth,
May melt in anguish, and that brow
　Forget that it was once so smooth !

But when the world is most unkind,
　And Fortune's smiles most fickle prove,
Oh, in that hour be sure to find
　A shelter in thy brother's love !

And as each fast-revolving year
　Flits o'er our heads on rapid wing,
May each to each but prove more dear,
　And each to each the closer cling ;—

Until at last, when fades the day,
　We, journeying with heavenward eyes,
May see through twilight lone and gray
　The looming towers of Paradise !

A DREAM.

The day was waning in the western sky,
  Above his grave brooded the broadening sun;
The twilight's shadows lengthened far and nigh—
    Another day was done.

All calmly and serene the moon uprose
  After that day of tempest and of grief;
But yet the evening brought me no repose,
    The calm brought no relief!

Under my woe I staggered like to faint;
  My lot seemed harder than I well could bear;
Through the pale light went up my impassioned
    plaint—
    ' Give me surcease from care !'

I gazed from out my window on the red
  And radiant sky where sank the orb of light,
Then seized the book of a sweet bard and read
    His ' Voices of the Night.'

I read impetuously—I know not why,
  For the sweet words upon my spirit fell,
As in the desert bread fell from the sky
    To hungry Israel !

But darkness deepened, and the words grew dim
  And faded from my faint and fading sight ;
I closed mine eyes and slept, and psalm and hymn
    Mingled their mystic light :

And in that light I dreamed a dream.   Behold,
  Two female forms of wondrous beauty rare
Stood o'er me ! One was tall and pale and cold,
    And dark her flowing hair :

Her dark eyes shone beneath her darker veil
  Like twin stars mirrored in tempestuous sea :
Her form was queenly in its grace, and pale
    Her brow did seem to me :

She wore a sombre robe, from head to foot
  All fringed with purple fire and flakes of light ;
She spoke in voice as soft and sweet as lute,
    And said, ' My name is Night.'

I turned and looked upon the other form
  That stood so motionless and silent there,—
Her cheek was rosy bright, her blue eyes warm,
    And golden was her hair :

Clad in a flowing robe of snowy white,
   Bedecked with glimmering pearls and silver's
      sheen,
She stood beside the sombre, shadowy Night
      Like some sweet fairy queen!

Then spake the dark-eyed maiden in her low
   Soft tones : ' We heard your anguished cry,
And came to grant thee respite from thy woe,—
      My sister Peace and I.

' We came from our sweet home afar to bring
   Strength to thy soul to battle with its care :
The *fear* of trouble is its fiercest sting.
      Go forth, and not despair!

' Bear sorrow as the Great-hearts of the earth
   Bore theirs,—go forth and meet it as 'tis seen,
And lo! like moist mirage in desert's dearth,
      What seems has never been!

' Face troubles boldly, and they fly away!
   Keep thy heart pure, thy form and soul erect!
Be strong in knowing man is more than clay;
      Be strong in self-respect!

' Remember also there is One who knows
   All things, however faint, obscure, and dim :
He will not let a brave heart fail, nor those
      That firmly trust in Him!'

' Face troubles boldly, and they fly away !
Keep thy heart pure, thy form and soul erect !
Be strong in knowing man is more than clay ;
Be strong in self-respect !

Then Peace stooped down and murmured in mine
    ear
A soft sweet gush of silver-sounding words,
Like prattle of a brooklet calm and clear,
    Or song of summer birds.

And I lay in a speechless ecstasy,
    Drinking in all the sweet words of those twain,
Until I felt the soul-strength within me
    Quicken and live again!

At length the soft sounds faded from the sense,
    The silence woke me, and I gazed afar
From out my window on the broad immense
    Of sky and shimmering star.

And there I sat and pondered o'er my dream,
    While stern Resolve came to my fainting soul,
Till through the troublous clouds there shone a
    gleam
    That showed a glorious goal!

The morrow dawned and died into the night;
    And with it came and went the fierce array
Of troubles that seemed coming like a blight
    To crush, destroy, and slay!

They passed like mist before the breath of morn,
  Teaching the stern realities of life;
Showing the fate of every creature born
    With care and woe is rife!

And as I sat and felt the perfumed air
  That hovered round that dreaded day's decease,
I breathed a blessing on the holy pair—
    Night and her sister Peace!

WHAT SHALL I SING?

WHAT shall I sing?   The life of things
   Is hidden from me by a cloud.
   Nothing is known.   The moving crowd
Are full of vain imaginings!

Some simple song at random sung—
   A tale to make the tear-drop start:—
   Vague thoughts are struggling in my heart,
But find no utterance on my tongue!

The thought that all the world commands—
   That far into the future dips;
   The poetry of clinging lips;
The poetry of clasping hands;

The throbbing joys that thrill the soul
   With deepest, wildest ecstasies;
   The longings that like troubled seas
Across the gulf of Being roll;—

All these I've known and tasted long,
    But cannot give them forth in words;
    I make a trembling 'mong the chords,
But cannot catch the soul of song.

When will the dew drop from the sky
    To slake the soul's undying thirst?
    When will this pent-up spirit burst
Forth in one flood of melody?.

A THOUGHT.

IF flowers could always bloom at eve
    As sweetly as they bloom at morn;
If joys could ne'er take wing and leave
    Our hearts to languish all forlorn :—
Then flowers would ne'er seem half so bright,
    And joys would ne'er be half so dear,—
The sweetest dawn of morning light
    Is that we gaze on through a tear !

FAREWELL TO THE YEAR 1861.

OLD YEAR, farewell; thy hours are swiftly flying,
    Thy sands are well-nigh run;
Old Year, we come to look upon thee dying,
    And welcome in thy son.

And as we see thy dim eyes slowly glazing,
    And hear thy labouring breath,
Thy voice no vain and useless protest raising
    Against the power of Death,

We almost wonder thus to see thee going
    So peaceful and serene,
When hearts are sad and eyes are overflowing
    For England's widowed Queen,

Whom thou hast ravished of her dearest treasure,
    Leaving her now to feel
A yearning want in every earthly pleasure,
    Which time can never heal.

Old Year, thy death-roll tells a mournful story
    Of useful lives removed ;
Forms have been crushed in manhood's pride and
      glory,
    And hearts are still that loved !

Old Year, above thy passing-bell's sad tolling,
    There sounds as from afar
The muttered under-tone of battle rolling,
    And thunder-note of war.

It comes across the broad Atlantic sweeping—
    That sound so wild and dread ;
'Tis heard above a mighty nation's weeping
    For *him* so lately dead.

And we must leave our peaceful avocations
    To battle for the right,
And prove that England's arm among the nations
    Has still the power to smite.

But, hark ! those bells of late chiming so sadly
    Again salute the ear :
Their silvery voices sounding sweetly, gladly,
    Ring in the fair New Year.

Oh, may those joy-bells be to us a token
　　Of what the year will be !
May England's hallowed peace remain unbroken,
　　Her people still be free !

Thus, though the Old Year is rung out with sorrow,
　　The new one is rung in
With joy, that speaks of many a bright to-morrow
　　When gladness shall begin

To take the place of grief, and cot and palace
　　Will hear the joyful strain,
And lips that long have pressed the bitter chalice
　　Shall taste the sweet again.

That over all this fair land, sea-surrounded,
　　The wail of woe may cease,
And the grim fiend of War may be confounded
　　By the sweet angel Peace.

THE HARP IS HUSHED.

The harp is hushed, its chords are still,
    No master hand has o'er them strayed ;
Perhaps not one responsive thrill
    Will meet these strains that I have made.

And yet I know my harp but waits
    The touch of a consummate hand,
To open wide song's treasure-gates,
    And scatter music o'er the land.

And though but weakly I have flung
    My trembling fingers o'er the strings,
Yet in these songs that I have sung
    There live the germs of greater things.

Then stay, my harp, and with me dwell,
    Until I learn the sacred art
To spread abroad song's magic spell,
    And flood with music every heart.

POEMS.

1862—1865.

1862—1865.

ON MY TWENTY-FIRST BIRTHDAY.

(February 3, 1862.)

I'M twenty-one : the spring-time has gone by,
  And now the summer of my life comes on ;
The short-lived summer that will fade and die
  As swiftly as the fair glad spring has gone.

But oh, to leave the fields where I have played,
  To join the world's eternal jar and strife !
And oh, to leave the streamlet in the glade,
  To mingle with the roaring sea of life !

I view the record of my bygone days—
  The blotted pages tell a mournful tale:
Of murmurs, where there was more need for
        praise ;
  Of failures, where a brave heart could not fail !

What have I done these one-and-twenty years
  That I should still encumber thus the ground ?
There falls no answer from the hidden spheres,
  And from the silent earth there comes no sound.

Yet, though the seasons of my faded youth
  Have failed in that which makes even Duty
    great,
O Lord, I thank Thee that I know this truth,
  " They also serve who only stand and wait."

THE CARRIER-PIGEON.

(An Answer to the Poem of that name by Dora Greenwell, in *Good Words* for February, 1862.)

ALL rosy bright the sun
    Sinks in the crimson glory of the west;
And tired workers now, their labour done,
    Betake themselves to rest.

The twilight shadows fall,
    And silence waits upon the fading day;
And in the summer woods the songsters all
    Have ceased their evening lay.

Then wherefore dost thou stay?
    Cleave with swift wing the incense-breathing
      air!
Come from the regions of the drooping day
    With that which thou dost bear.

6

My snow-white messenger !
   This hour I've watched the weary sun
    decline,
Thinking each moment that thy wings would
    stir
   The leafy jessamine :

That thou wouldst enter in—
   Thy snowy plumage ruffled on thy breast,
And perch upon my bosom, and begin
   To take thy well-earned rest.

And still thou art not here—
   The sun has sunk behind the woods afar,
And through the silver twilight, lone and clear,
   Looks forth the evening star.

I know that *he* doth sit
   Beside his open casement far away ;
O'er his pale brow the twilight shadows flit,
   As if at merry play;

The book is on his knee—
   He gazes far across the uplands dim ;
His thoughts are in the chamber *here* with me,
   While mine are *there* with him.

How wonderful is Thought
    When borne upon the rapid wings of Love!
'Tis with the spirit's deepest breathings fraught,
    And needs no Carrier Dove

To waft it through the air;
    The heart is flooded by its silent power;
As in dim summer dawns the dewdrops fair
    Refresh a thirsty flower!

But now thy journey's past,
    My pure-plumed messenger, and here thou
        art—
I've read his wished-for letter o'er at last,
    And pressed it to my heart;

And when a blissful thought
    Awakes me in the drowsy hours of night,
I'll kiss the letter o'er which thou hast brought
    Beneath thy pinions white.

My thanks I owe to thee,
    Thou ever-faithful messenger of Love,
Whose murmurous cooing speaks so tenderly,
    My gentle Carrier Dove!

A HUNDRED YEARS AGO.

THE Now into the Past is flitting,
    Never again to reappear ;
And solemn Death is ever sitting
    Beside the portal of each year ;
And man must also pass away,
    And leave this narrow sphere below :
None of those forms are here to-day
    That lived a hundred years ago.

Eyes that with love were overflowing,
    Hands that were warmly clasped in hands,
Hearts that with tenderness were glowing,
    Souls knit in pure affection's bands :—
All these have floated down the tide
    Of time, which runs with ceaseless flow,
And with them all the joy and pride
    That graced—a hundred years ago.

And o'er the lapse of years long faded
  We look upon the bygone days,—
The world by gloom and mist is shaded,
  And all is strange that meets our gaze :
We have no smiles to greet the mirth,
  No tears to mingle with the woe,
Of those who lived upon the earth
  More than a hundred years ago.

Yet every word which then was spoken,
  And every thought that wrung the brow
And strove for utterance faint and broken,
  Exert an influence on the Now—
An influence which for ever throws
  Its power o'er all, and serves to show
That we are kindred still to those
  Who lived a hundred years ago.

Then wherefore should we still endeavour
  To mar the wise and God-like plan
Which strives to prove to us for ever
  The brotherhood of man to man ?
A thousand echoes ringing loud,
  A thousand voices whispering low,
Tell what we owe unto the crowd
  Who lived a hundred years ago.

STARVED.

THE deep night fell o'er London,
  With its riot and bustle and din—
It fell o'er the streets of the city;
  It fell o'er the haunts of sin.
Were there none with hearts of pity
  To take the poor wayfarer in?

She walked through Christian London,
  Wretched, bare-footed, forlorn;
With pleading, hunger-pinched features—
  With aspect weary and worn;
And the wild March blast, as it hurried past,
  Fluttered her raiment torn.

' No home in all wide London !
She shrank from the chilly air ;
She drew her tattered mantle
Round her shoulders cold and bare.'

No home in all wide London !
  She shrank from the chilly air ;
She drew her tattered mantle
  Round her shoulders cold and bare,
And from the beat of the rain and sleet
  She crouched on the lonely stair.

And through the streets of London
  The heedless crowd went on ;
No eye saw the friendless woman,
  No ear heard her piteous moan ;
No kindly heart that was human
  Cared for the homeless one !

Death stalked through the streets of London,
  But less unkind was he ;
He saw the woman lying
  In her lonesome misery :
He took her hand, and in accents bland
  Said, ' Come along with me !'

Day dawned on stately London !
  The sun shone warm and bright
On the woman's crouching figure,
  In its melancholy plight—
On her garments torn and meagre,
  On her features still and white.

Starved in the streets of London !
   Yet mayhap a mother has smiled
In the old-time days of happiness
   In the laughing eyes of a child ;—
Those eyes that now glare with a stony stare,
   And gleam with a radiance wild.

Starved in the streets of London—
   Midst its wealth and the ceaseless swell
Of its trade and its commerce rising high
   To the heavens ! O ye who dwell
In the midst of riches and luxury,
   Say—Is it well ? is it well ?

AN OLD MAN'S LOVE SONG.

Do you forget the joyous time
    When summer woods were green and palmy?
When we were in our youthful prime,
    And summer days were bright and balmy?
Then wandering through the wooded ways,
    Or couched among the purple heather,
Screened from the sun's refulgent rays,
    We sang our merry songs together.

Glad was the time : no carking care
    Had ever cast a shadow o'er us ;
The path we trod was bright and fair,
    And life lay bright and fair before us.
So, hand in hand, we journeyed on
    With hearts as light as any feather :
Life had a sunny side alone,
    When you and I sang songs together.

Those days seem far, far distant now—
　The way we've wandered long and dreary—
The furrows gather on your brow,
　And I am growing worn and weary;
Along the path that we have trod
　We've met dark clouds and stormy weather,
And over many an Ichabod
　We've wept our burning tears together.

Yet, close together, as of old,
　Across the waste we'll still keep moving;
Years cannot make our hearts grow cold,
　Age cannot keep these hearts from loving.
And when we leave this world of care,
　Then, far above yon floating ether,
In that bright land where all is fair
　We'll sing our joyful songs together.

MAY DAY, 1862.

Glad voices o'er the land
  Ring in loud shouts of joy and thankfulness,
For, laurel-crowned by Plenty, Peace doth stand
  This happy day to bless.

This day the nations meet—
  Not as of old they met, in warfare rude,
But every clime is linked in friendship sweet
  And bonds of brotherhood.

And in one stately hall,
  Thronged with the triumphs of man's soaring
        mind,
No single separate race is owned, but all
  Are members of mankind ;

And as the voice of praise
  Rings through the corridors and fails again,
Angels are singing as in olden days,
  ' Peace and goodwill to men !'

A blessing on *his* name
　　Whose mind conceived this world-embracing
　　　　plan
Of universal love, which shows the claim
　　Man ever holds on man :—

Whose unobtrusive life
　　Was one still struggle in the cause of peace,
To hasten on the golden day when strife
　　And enmity shall cease.

A tear for *her* who yet
　　Mourns for the chosen of her youthful years—
The royal widow, in her deep regret,
　　Victoria in her tears.

She weeps for him who stood
　　So long the partner of her happy reign :
O pathos of her splendid solitude !
　　O passion of her pain !

Yet though her eyes are dim
　　With tears, a joy must thrill her soul to-day,
To see crowned with success the work of him,
　　Her Great-heart, passed away.

Our Albert ! lo, the whole
　　Wide world unites thy monument to rear,
And in this hall of nations every soul
　　Doth hold thy memory dear.

Behold, it is the May!
   Her voice awakens all the vernal flowers ;
The woods put on their verdure fresh and gay,
   And vocal are the bowers.

The perfume-laden breeze
   Creeps faintly o'er the land like incense mild ;
A thousand birds sing from a thousand trees
   With carol sweet and wild ;

And as the voice of praise
   Swells upward to the sky and fails again,
Angels are singing as in olden days,
   ' Peace and goodwill to men !'

WHITBY ABBEY.

Thou relic of a bygone generation,
  Thou crumbling record of a vanished race,
Towering aloft in lonely desolation,
  Like the great guardian spirit of the place :

Thy walls with age are mouldering, gray and hoary,
  Where thy long transept lay the grass waves
    green,
And scarce a remnant of thy former glory
  Remains to tell us what thou once hast been.

Yet here in days of yore a royal maiden
  Has ministered upon the sacred shrine ;
And knights and nobles with their symbols laden
  Have joined the orisons and rites divine.

Here images of saints in dark-niched spaces
  Have peered on black-cowled monks devoid of
    smiles ;
And meek-eyed nuns, with fair and pensive faces,
  Have flitted through the solemn-whispering
    aisles.

Here oft the sweet strains of an Ave Mary
   Have stolen through the twilight, still and clear;
And the wild cadence of a Miserere
   Has struck upon the midnight's startled ear.

And in the frequent pauses of devotion,
   When silence brooded o'er the prostrate band,
Was heard the deep-mouthed wailing of the ocean
   Beating for ever on the rocky strand.

But all is changed!—no more the night-wind, stealing
   Through thy dim galleries and vacant nave,
Will catch the sound of music's measured pealing
   And bear it far across the moon-lit wave;

No more when morning gilds the eastern heaven
   Will early matins rise or organ swell;
And when the first stars gem the brow of even
   No more will sound the sweet-toned vesper bell.

Thy glory has gone by! and thou art standing
   In lonely pomp upon the sea-washed hill,
Wearing in hoary age a mien commanding,
   And in thy desolation stately still!

EIGHTEEN HUNDRED AND SIXTY-TWO.

If, ages after this, when I
    Have long been lying 'neath the clover,
These lines should chance to meet the eye
    Of one who'll deign to read them over,—

Mortal, I fain would speak with you
    Awhile in this imperfect sonnet,
Of life in eighteen-sixty-two—
    How the ' world wagged ' when I was on it.

In History's statements put no trust—
    Historians never are impartial ;
If you read novels, know you must
    That these at best are merely farcial :

But mine will be a faithful tale
    Of simple truth, I do assure you—
No scenes to make your cheeks turn pale,
    No far-fetched fancies to allure you.

I scarce know how in words to mould
  The struggling thoughts that o'er me gather;
Yet list, and I'll ' a tale unfold '
  As long as that of Hamlet's father.

Of course, in eighteen-sixty-two
  We had not all *your* privileges,
For Art's deep Ocean, broad and blue,
  Was only spanned by floating-bridges;

And we were ' cabined, cribbed, confined,'
  A rude convention kept us under;
We chained the lightning, bound the wind,
  But never knew the use of thunder!

Eight days our steamboats took to plough
  The Atlantic 'gainst the storm-king's powers—
Why speak of this ?   No doubt you now
  Can cross it in as many hours !

In naval warfare we excelled—
  It was no use our ships to fire on ;
Armstrong and Whitworth guns they held ;
  Their hulls were coated o'er with iron.

We learned the secrets of the stars,
  Explored the wonders of the ocean,
Burst Education's prison bars,
  And set her glorious car in motion.

But not content with what we knew
    Of all the varied spheres of science—
In theory and practice too—
    With other worlds we sought alliance !

We summoned ghosts in number more
    Than those that came to blood-stained Gloster;
To hear from friends lost years before,
    We'd but to go to Mr. Foster !

The way they came no tongue could tell,
    On chairs and stools they used to hammer—
Most had forgot the way to spell,
    And very few could speak good grammar !

The ghost of Walter Scott told lies !
    But then in life *he* loved romancing :
Heber was given to cards and dice,
    And Dr. Watts was fond of dancing !

And all this time great Science strode
    With giant strides, we slowly following,
Though oft with open mouths we stood
    Some grand delusive fiction swallowing.

Of locomotion I'll not make
    My tale to tell, or you'll not scan it,
Since I've no doubt you now can take
    A journey to some distant planet !

Of mighty Love we owned the sway;
   We felt the stormy glow of passion ;
We slept all night; we woke all day;
   We dressed—in the prevailing fashion.

We harboured hate and joy and fear;
   We courted—ah ! you know what that is :
A tale told in a trellised ear,
   Beside a trellised window lattice.

We went to church on Sabbath days,
   When solemn Sabbath bells were ringing ;—
Some went to gaze—some went to praise—
   Some went ' because they liked the singing.'

In riches and in luxury
   Thousands of wealthy men were lying ;
While, steeped in abject misery,
   As many more of want were dying.

Yet still, amidst Want's piercing moan,
   And busy Labour's ceaseless humming,
We thought that Joy was hastening on,
   And that a better time was coming.

Dreaming we ever could behold,
   Beyond the midnight's misty covering,
A happy daybreak, fringed with gold,
   Upon the verge of darkness hovering !

Fools ! thus we let the years glide by,
    Nor dreamed that they had most of beauty,
Who, spite of Hope's delusive cry,
    Strongly and nobly did their duty.

We seldom thought the solemn Past
    Spread its far-stretching shadow o'er us ;
Or that the Future, wide and vast,
    Lay an untrodden waste before us !

We lived as if the world at best
    Were but a place of mere transition,
Nor ever deemed that each possessed
    In his own sphere a special mission.

Farewell, my friend ! the silent night
    Is slowly falling, dim and dimmer,
And through the weird and lonely light
    I see your unborn features glimmer !

I seem to grasp your ghostly hand !
    All outer human things are banished !
The Dawn comes creeping o'er the land,
    And, lo ! thy shadowy form has vanished !

LOVELY IN DEATH.

STILL, still and lovely, as some sculptured form,
　She lay draped in her shroud of snowy white;
But cold the cheek that once was purely warm,
　And dim the eye that once was proudly bright.

The rich curl-clusters of her golden hair
　Hung o'er the pulseless form in careless grace;
And Death's cold shadow rested on the fair
　And placid beauty of the faultless face.

The parted lips still wore a ruby tinge,
　And round the mouth a smile yet seemed to play;
The right hand rested on the curtain-fringe,
　As if in deep and dreamless sleep she lay:

And once or twice when the faint summer breeze
　Fluttered the golden glory of her hair,
Hope smiled above our gathering miseries,
　And 'Death,' we said, 'cannot be dwelling there!'

But when the twilight fell in hazy gloom,
  And 'neath the window sang the wakeful bird,
A silent horror brooded o'er the room,
  And all the fountains of our being stirred;

' And she is gone,' we said, ' for ever gone!
  That silvery voice can now be heard no more!
No more those half-closed eyes shall meet our own,
  Their dark-blue depths with warm love running
      o'er!'

And a wild hunger seized upon our hearts
  For all the joys possessed in days of old;
The clinging lips—where all the life-blood starts;
  The clasping hands—where neither hand is cold.

Then as the solemn night chased twilight gray,
  We felt a softening influence hovering nigh:
We said, ' Our darling has not gone away;
  She is not dead, although she seemed to die.

' She still is in our midst, though years may roll,
  And life be blown away by every breath:
For beauty is immortal as the soul;
  And Love can never yield her crown to Death!'

THE TRYSTING TREE.

WE stood beneath the trysting tree
  One summer evening long ago ;
The leaves were rustling drowsily,
  The air was still, the sun was low ;

The songsters in the woods were dumb,
  No sound came from the breezy down ;
But, faint and deep, a ceaseless hum
  Rose upward from the crowded town.

Her hand I held within mine own ;
  I saw her bosom fall and rise,
While lovingly upon me shone
  The sunshine splendour of her eyes.

And standing in the twilight there,
  I carved her name upon the tree ;
She loosed the night of her long hair.
  And gave a silken tress to me.

I hid the token in my breast,
My heart leaped up with sudden joy,
And in wild words my tongue confessed
The first love-passion of a boy.

Ah me! the deep tumultuous bliss
That thrilled my bosom when I felt
Her stooping down to print a kiss
Upon my forehead as I knelt!

And then I vowed though her dear name
Might fade from off the gnarléd tree,
My love would still remain the same,
And I would never faithless be!

So home we sauntered, while the night
Hung all its star-lamps out on high,
And the moon framed with tremulous light
A silver pathway to the sky.

But often when the leafy wood
Was wrapt in shadowy gloom, I came
To see the place where she had stood
And kiss the letters of her name.

Her love I cherished in my soul,
And deemed that it would ever bloom
In life, and through the years that roll
Their endless course beyond the tomb!

'And standing in the twilight there,
I carved her name upon the tree;
She loosed the night of her long hair,
And gave a silken tress to me.'

But, oh! the world is full of change!
  And boyhood's days glide swiftly by;
Our early loves grow cold and strange,
  And all youth's bright enchantments fly.

The other day again I stood
  Where passed my boyhood wild and free;
I left the town, and sought the wood,
  And found the well-remembered tree:

All seemed the same. The woods were dumb,
  No sound came from the breezy down,
But faint and deep, a drowsy hum
  Rose upward from the crowded town:—

And standing there, I thought, 'Ah me!
  How soon from youth's fond joys we part!'
The name was blotted from the tree;
  The love had withered from my heart.

THE SEA.

WHAT ails thee, O thou Sea,
　That thus with mad endeavour
Thou heavest thy waves on the lonely shore,
　And beatest thy banks for ever ?

Ah ! so my weary heart
　Throbs with a restless yearning,
For the golden light of the faded days,
　And the joys that have no returning.

What means, O tossing Sea,
　That wild and awful wailing,
Like the prayer for pity from some lost soul
　Which is ever unavailing ?

Oh, even so my heart
　Doth wail, and pine, and languish,
For a love that can satisfy the soul,
　And a peace that can still its anguish.

Wail wilder still, O Sea !
  Roar louder yet, ye billows !
And rock the mariners to sleep
  As they rest on their lonely pillows !

And heave on high thy waves
  Till the deep shall seethe and shiver !
But a day will come when thy wail shall cease,
  And thy moan shall be hushed for ever !

And thou, O restless heart,
  Still throb with thy deep emotion ;
And pine beneath thy weight of care,
  And pant like the panting ocean ;

And toss and tremble and thrill
  Till thine inmost being quiver !
But a day will come when thy care shall cease,
  And thou shalt be stilled for ever !

'HOW WILT THOU DO IN THE SWEL-
LING OF JORDAN?'

(Jeremiah xii. 8.)

FAINT not, O Christian! the way may be long,
   And the path for thy feet may seem toilsome
      and weary;
Courage, and faint not; be faithful and strong:
   Though days may be dark, and though nights
      may be dreary.
Onward! though mists rise on every hand:
   Upward! though sin weigh thee down like a
      burden:
For if thou shouldst faint in the still peaceful
   land,
   'How wilt thou do in the swelling of Jordan?'

Faint not, O Christian! the night is far spent,
   And the day will soon dawn in its fulness of
      beauty:

Let the light find thee with steps heavenward bent,
  Toiling along the rough pathway of duty!
What though temptations are thronging the road!
  Has not Christ died thy transgressions to
    pardon?
And if thou shouldst wander away from thy God,
  'How wilt thou do in the swelling of Jordan?'

Faint not, O Christian! though thick on thy path
  Affliction pour down its most pitiless showers:
Thy Father is speaking in love, not in wrath,
  And thy griefs will yet scatter thy pathway like
    flowers!
Courage then, Christian! be of good cheer!
  Christ is thy Guardian and heaven is thy
    guerdon!
For if on this earth thou shouldst falter and fear,
  'How wilt thou do in the swelling of Jordan?

GOD IS EVERYWHERE.

Mountains, towering high and proud,
Far above each floating cloud ;
Forests, 'mong whose crowded trees,
Moans the frequent midnight breeze ;
Ocean, with its solemn roar,
Lashing on the lonely shore ;
Thunder echoing through the air,—
Tell us, God is everywhere !

Flowers of every scent and hue
Pearly with the morning dew ;
Lake whose limpid bosom heaves
In the light that sunset leaves ;
Stars that shine so stilly bright
From the azure vault of night ;
Sunshine with its beauteous glare,—
Tell us, God is everywhere !

Spring, with all the flow'rets sweet
Leaping forth to kiss her feet;
Summer, with her foliage gay,
And the roses on her way;
Autumn, with his purple skies
And the passion in his eyes;
Winter, with his woodlands bare,—
Tell us, God is everywhere!

Birds that trill their happy lays
All along the wooded ways;
Leaves that rustle far aloft,
Making music sweet and soft;
Streamlet of the silvery tones
Prattling o'er its smooth gray stones;
With all sounds of beauty rare,—
Tell us, God is everywhere!

Visions of the morning light;
Dreams that haunt us in the night;
Shadowy hands that beckon hence;
Whisperings we know not whence;
Hopes that wear angelic wings;
Beautiful imaginings;
Yearnings after all things fair,—
Tell us, God is everywhere!

Courage then, O fainting heart,
Worn and weary as thou art !
What though earthly joys fall fast
As the leaves in Autumn's blast !
What though seas of trouble roll
Billowy darkness o'er thy soul !
Thou canst crush the phantom Care,
While thy God is everywhere !

When the shadows round thee fall
Blacker than a funeral pall ;
When the tempest's brooding wrath
Bursts upon thy lonely path ;
In all days of deep distress ;
In all hours of loneliness,—
Bend the knee and breathe the prayer,—
For thy God is everywhere !

CALM AND STORM.

'Tis only when the ocean lies
  In undisturbed and waveless sleep,
No breath beneath the bending skies,
  No ripple on the spreading deep,—
Nothing to mar its slumb'rous rest,
  No fleck upon its limpid blue,
That, in its broad and placid breast,
  Heaven is reflected pure and true.

So with the heart of human-kind:
  'Tis only when in perfect rest,
No cloud of doubt upon the mind,
  No dream of ill within the breast,—
The conscience clear, the faith secure,
  Each thought the pinion of a prayer,
Each aspiration high and pure,
  That heaven is softly mirrored there.

Yet, even when the tempests sweep
   Tumultuous o'er the tossing sea,
And all the furies of the deep
   Meet in uproarious revelry;
When wild winds rage, and ocean raves,
   And thunder-black each billow seems,
Still heaven is mirrored 'neath the waves
   In broken and disjointed gleams!

So is it with the heart of man:
   When tempests howl and waves are high;
When faith is growing pale and wan,
   And hope's last beam about to die;
No promised calm the soul to cheer,
   By winds of passion tossed and driven:—
E'en then, beneath the storms, appear
   Distorted gleams and hints of heaven!

AWAKE.

THE sun is flooding the eastern sky
  With a blaze of silver light !
The fresh green foliage, waving high,
  Is fringed with a flame of white ;
And far above, from the topmost air,
  The showering lark-notes break ;
And the spirit of beauty floats everywhere—
  Sweet my lady, awake !

A slow breeze steals o'er the dewy land,
  From its home in the dreamy South,
And scatters a perfume on every hand
  As sweet as the breath of your mouth ;
And the tremulous boughs, as they bend and sway,
  A murmurous music make ;
And bright on the brooklet the sunbeams play—
  Sweet my lady, awake !

The river that lay in its dusky repose
  Through the long lone hours of night,
Now laughs in the lustre that sunrise throws,
  And ripples in rosy light ;
And the hills that loomed like shadowy ghosts
  A clearer outline take ;
And the white sails glimmer along the coasts—
  Dear my lady, awake !

The violet lifts its eye of blue
  To the bending blue above ;
And the roses, bathed in a drench of dew,
  Are breathing of beauty and love ;
And the lily stoops its head to kiss
  Its shadow within the lake—
Oh, never was morning so lovely as this !
  Dear my lady, awake !

Awake ! for a music is flooding the air,
  And melting along the deep.
When nature is all awake and so fair,
  Oh, why should my lady sleep ?
A passionate sigh begins to start
  From the depth of each thicket and brake—
A sigh that finds echo within my heart—
  Oh, sweet my lady, awake !

Awake! and come where the zephyr moves
  In ripples across the grass:
Awake! and come to the lake that loves
  To mirror your form as you pass;
And come, oh, come, to the heart that pines
  And languishes for your sake;
And bright eyes shall blind each dewdrop that
    shines—
  Dear my lady, awake!

'COR UNUM, VIA UNA.'

Man's heart doth ever tend towards the right :
    We cannot wander from the Perfect Way,
But inward voices whisper in their might,—
    Thy feet are turned astray !

No heart but sometimes feels remorseful pangs,
    When passion holds its empire, fierce and wild,
Nor bends in sorrow as a mother hangs
    Above her wayward child.

No eye so stolid but a tear will steal
    Out of its chambers with resistless force ;
No heart so stony that it will not feel
    The meltings of remorse !

And all men yet, however fallen and base,
    Possess some traits of true nobility ;
The heart still whispers from its secret place,
    All they were meant to be !

And knowing this, it is my hope that all
   Shall yet fulfil the human heart's desire,
And in some region, free from earthly thrall,
   May labour and aspire.

One God to wipe away all guilt and tears !
   One hope to nerve the mind and soothe the
      breast !
One Heart to guide through all the deathless
      years !
   One Way that leads to rest !

MARCH 10TH, 1863.

RISE, Morning, from thine orient bed,
  By spring-time breezes softly fanned ;
Come, happy Daybreak, gently led
  By Hope and Joy, across the land.

Let sunshine bathe thy beauteous wing,
  Thy form be decked with fairest flowers ;
And let thine incense-breathings bring
  A whisper of the summer hours.

Hush all thy hoarse winds into calm ;
  No shadow o'er thy features start ;
But let thy beauty break like balm
  Of joy upon the nation's heart.

Linger in sweetness everywhere,
  But drop thy choicest influence down
Where Denmark's daughter, young and fair,
  Weds with the heir of England's crown,

And two young hearts with hope elate
  Upon life's sunny threshold stand,
About to pass the golden gate
  Into the future, hand in hand.

A year has scarcely passed away
  Since all the land was wrapt in gloom,
And grief's long shadow brooding lay
  In blackness over Albert's tomb.

Then all the splendour of the throne
  Was hidden by a cloud of woe,
And each heart felt that grief its own
  Which bent the Monarch's head so low

But now a ray of promise comes
  Resplendent o'er the Northern Sea,
To scatter sorrow's lurking glooms,
  And bid the darkness cease to be ;

And England looks with lively hope
  To see the shadows flit away,
O Morn, when thy rich gates shall ope,
  And dawn shall widen into day.

O father of our future King,
  Whose voice on earth is silent now ;
Whose late-known virtues serve to fling
  Intenser glory round thy brow ;

Stoop from thy high and radiant place,
   And breathe upon our Prince to-day
That love and hope and earnestness
   Which charmed and graced thine own brief
     stay :

That he to royalty may give
   A glory earthly gloss above ;
That he may live as thou didst live ;
   That he may love as thou didst love !

Then, happy Morn, shine sweetly down !
   Pour forth thy wealth of golden rays !
And in a flood of sunshine drown
   The memory of the winter days !

And whilst the young, fond, loving pair
   Pronounce the sacred bridal troth,
With glad acclaim we'll fill the air,
   And pray for blessings on them both ;

That joy may on their path be found,
   Whilst duty leads them in the way,
And that their life, by warm love crowned,
   May prove one long, long wedding-day !

THE LEAF OF WOODRUFF.

I FOUND a leaf of woodruff in a book :
    Gone was its scent, and lost its pristine glory ;
Each slender bladelet wore a dingy look,
    And all was blanched and hoary.

And yet this withered leaf a spell possessed,
    Which worked upon me in mysterious measure,
And sent old memories thronging through my
      breast
    Of mingled pain and pleasure.

Of childhood's days that knew no thought of care ;
    Of hours that passed on wings of rainbow fleet-
      ness ;
Of odours floating on the wanton air
    Sad from their very sweetness ;

Of woods that wore a garb of summer green ;
    Of knee-deep ferns, and nooks of shady stillness ;
Of streams that glimmered in the full moon's sheen,
    And mirrored back its fulness ;

Of lazy baskings on the lone hillside
  In the fierce glow of July's sultry weather ;
Of twilight wanderings where the enamoured tide
  Crept up to kiss the heather ;

Of voices still beneath the churchyard sod ;
  Bright eyes that glistened from behind long
      lashes ;
Warm beauty early given back to God ;
  Red lips that now are ashes !

And many other memories, gay and grave,
  The woodruff brought in life-like guise before
      me ;
Until I marvelled how a leaf could have
  Such magic influence o'er me.

Ah, so it is ! all that hath ever been
  Experienced by the spirit is immortal ;
Each hope and joy and grief is hid within
  The memory's sacred portal.

And yet the soft glow of a moonlight hour,
  A strain of haunting music sweet and olden,
A dream, a bird, a bee, a leaf, a flower,
  A sunset rich and golden,

'Of twilight wanderings where the enamoured tide
Crept up to kiss the heather.'

Can fling that portal open ; and beyond
    Appears the record of each earlier feeling ;—
All hopes, all joys, all fears, all musings fond,
    In infinite revealing :

Till all the present passes from the sight—
    Its cares and woes that make us weary-hearted,
And leaves us basking in the holy light
    Of golden days departed.

MINE.

Oh, let me love thee, for my life is lonely,
  And fain my heart would hang its faith on thine ;
My soul would thrill with wildest joy, if only
  It knew and felt thee mine.

Mine, only mine, to prize with warm devotion,
  And cherish with a lover's ceaseless care ;
To smooth this rough world's path of rude com-
    motion
  And make it bright and fair.

Mine, only mine, in joy as well as sorrow,
  Thy pure heart free from every taint of guile,
To drink fresh hope from those sweet eyes, and
    borrow
  New courage from thy smile.

Mine, only mine, for ever and for ever,
  Warm hand in hand, and faithful heart to heart,
In bonds that time is all too weak to sever,
  And death must fail to part !

Mine midst the clanging din, the 'wildering rattle,
  The glory of this stern world's strife begun;
Mine in the hazy tumult of the battle;
  Mine when the victory's won!

Mine when this reeling earth is racked and
     quivering,
  And worlds are tottering on the verge of night:
Mine when the host of stars, pallid and shivering,
  Refuse to yield their light!

Mine through eternity's unnumbered ages,
  In the hereafter world of light and bliss,
Where never sorrow reigns, nor tempest rages,
  Nor hearts ache, as in this!

Then let me love thee, for my heart is straining
  To fly away and rest itself on thine;
And, passion-tossed, my spirit is complaining,—
  Oh, let thy love be mine!

No heart was made for loneliness or sadness—
  Some other beats with true responsive thrill;
And love, though given all vainly and in madness,
  Is sweet and holy still.

It is my faith that those who purely cherish
  True love, no matter whether crowned or
    crossed,
Unite in that bright realm where grief must
    perish,
  But nothing pure is lost.

Then, if not here, perhaps in those high regions,
  In the great shadow of the eternal throne,
I'll single thee from all the shining legions,
  And claim thee as mine own.

When those brown tresses wave in richer splen-
    dour,
  Far from the wasting breath of earthly years,
And those large eyes, so lustrous and so tender,
  Shall never dim with tears.

Behold, a glory purples all the meadows!
  Thoughts rise as pure as childhood's happy
    dreams,
And through the twilight's gray far-folded shadows
  Heaven's starry radiance gleams.

THE CLOUD.

I SAW a little lonely cloud
    Hung on the western verge of heaven ;
In twilight's earliest beams it glowed,
    And mirrored back the blush of even ;
No other cloud was in the sky,
It lay in lonely witchery.

The twilight deepened : one by one
    The pale stars trembled through the haze ;
The golden light of eve was gone,
    And gone the sunset's lingering blaze ;
Yet still that little cloudlet lay,
In mellow beauty, softly gay.

A silence brooded far and nigh,
    A stillness burdened all the air,
And the wide welkin stretched on high
    In dusky azure everywhere,—
Save that one spot, where, earthward bowed,
Stooped down the solitary cloud !

It looked so lovely as it lay
    Becalmed upon the waveless blue,
Its border melting, faintly gray,
    Into the sky's diviner hue;
And yet, I know not how nor why,
It brought the teardrop to my eye!

And ever when I think upon
    That cloud on the horizon's rim,
Brooding in beauty, rich and lone—
    My heart is sad, my eyes grow dim,
And I could long to fly away,
To where the little cloudlet lay.

'Tis ever thus! the spirit pants
    For all things peaceful, fair and sweet;
For joys that leave no aching wants;
    For bliss that is not incomplete!
But all these yearnings vague and fond
Must anchor in the great Beyond.

GLENCOE.

Mountain-top o'er mountain rising,
  Crag o'er crag, and steep o'er steep,
Rugged scenes the heart surprising,
  With an awe profound and deep;
Mountain streamlets gliding onward
  With a swift unceasing flow,
Rushing, pouring, hurrying downward
  To the rivulet below,
Which in mellow music surges
  All its rocky channels through:
And along the mountain gorges
  Frequent peeps of heavenly blue.
All around the waving heather,
  And the rocks so stern and brown;
Somewhere from the far-off ether
  Dulcet lark-notes dropping down:
On yon crag a raven perching,
  And a mist-cloud, wave on wave,
Brooding like some ghostly arching
  O'er the mouth of Ossian's cave.

And I sit and watch the gushing
　Of the little rivulet,
With its crystal waters rushing
　On in ceaseless foam and fret;
Beetling crags o'erhanging lonely
　Caverns wrapt in thunder-gloom,
Where the mountain-eagle only
　In their shadow finds a home;
Rocks upraised like stately columns;
　Passes where the wild wind plays;—
I can read them all like volumes
　Filled with tales of vanished days.

'Tis a morning in September,
And a breeze steals down the hill,
Sending all at once a chill
Through the frame, and I remember
I am sitting in Glencoe—
With its scenery enchanting,
With its crags and streamlets haunting—
And my fancy wanders back
To that morning long ago,
When, across the frozen snow,
Echoed o'er the mountains black
Warriors' curses uttered plainly,
Women's voices pleading vainly,
Yells and shouts and frantic crying,

Clanging shocks of angry steel,
And, dealt above the dead and dying,
Blows which strong arms only deal!
I can hear the deadly mutter
From between the clenchèd teeth,
And upon the snow-clad heath,
Up those hills which darkness drape,
I can see the ghostly flutter
Of woman's clothing in the wind,
Striving vainly to escape
From the home she leaves behind,
Where so calmly she lay sleeping
Only one short hour ago,
And never dreamed that death was keeping
Watch o'er misery-doomed Glencoe!
I behold the figures looming
Strangely through the dusky morning,
And I hear the hollow booming
Of the firelocks of the Campbells,
Striving other sounds to drown,
As, without a word of warning,
Brave McIon is struck down
Like a bullock at the shambles!
Unworthy of the land of Bruce!
Traitor Campbells! who could lose
In the memory of a feud
All that chivalrous respect

Which your sires were wont to show
To an unarmed, trusting foe :
On women's heads your vengeance wreaked,
In childhood's blood your hands imbued,
And—shamed by those of savage life—
Making the sacred name of *guest*
A passport to a kinsman's breast,
In which to plunge the assassin's knife !

Slumb'rous peace and awful silence
    Brood above this valley now,
As if never sounds of violence
    Thrilled its echoing gorges through ;
Gone the clang of warfare glorious ;
    Hushed the pibroch in the glen ;
Perished all the wild, uproarious
    Noise and tramp of armèd men !
Desolation without measure !
    No sweet homestead here and there ;
No fair cottage with its azure
    Smoke-wreath rising through the air !
No home sounds to follow after
    Wild-goat's bleat or eaglet's wail—
Childhood's voice or girlish laughter
    Echoing through the quiet vale !
In one spot the ruins only
    Of the homes of murdered men

Make the loneliness more lonely,
  Add a weirdness to the glen :
And vague thoughts of awful mystery
  Overwhelm me like a blast,
Blowing from the page of History
  All the horrors of the Past—
As I view the phantoms flitting
  From their graves of long ago,
And remember I am sitting
  In the valley of Glencoe.

THE SEASONS.

O Morn ! by softest breezes fanned,
  Pour down thy sunlight in a flood !
The Spring is laughing o'er the land,
  And dancing in my blood !
I clasp a warm hand, soft and fair,
  A strange wild joy my bosom swells ;
And floats upon the happy air
    The chime of marriage-bells.

The Summer sky in beauty glows ;
  The Summer breezes murmur light ;
And, underneath the blossoming rose,
  The dews are glistening bright.
And Summer, fair in every part,
  A thing of joy to me has grown,—
I feel the love-warmth of a heart
    That beats against mine own !

The leaves are falling sere and dead ;
  Hushed is the Summer's gladsome hum ;
The Summer flowers their bloom have shed,
  And Autumn-time has come.
The light has passed from sea and shore,
  These days are not the days of old ;
  hold the hand I held of yore,
  But, ah ! its clasp is cold !

O wind of Winter, rave and blow ;
  Sweep wildly o'er each crested wave !
Howl up the slopes across the snow,
  But pause upon her grave !
Wail sadly there : then onward start
  With louder gust and wilder moan !—
The joy hath perished from my heart,
  And I go forth alone !

'PEACE, BE STILL.'

WHEN the clouds loom dark and eerie,
   And the heavens are fraught with ill,
Flesh is weak and heart is weary—
   Saviour, whisper, ' Peace be still.'

When the mighty storm is surging,
   Stars are hid and winds are shrill,
Satan striving, passion urging—
   Saviour, whisper, ' Peace, be still.'

When the waves of Doubt and Terror
   Toss me at their own wild will,
Light seems dark and truth seems error—
   Saviour, whisper, ' Peace, be still.'

When affliction's storms are howling,
   And its voice my soul doth thrill,
Earth is black and heaven is scowling—
   Saviour, whisper, ' Peace, be still.'

'Saviour, whisper, " Peace, be still." '

When the shadows round me thicken,
   Bitter tears mine eyelids fill,
Spirit faints and senses sicken—
   Saviour, whisper, ' Peace, be still.'

When the tide of death's cold river
   Shocks me with its icy chill,
Body quakes and billows quiver—
   Saviour, whisper, ' Peace, be still.'

LIFE AND DEATH.

YOUNG Life came carolling over the earth ;
   Careless and happy and gay was he :—
Courting the sunshine in radiant mirth,
   Chasing the shadows in rosy glee :
Flowery and green was the path that he trode ;
   Fair sky above him and bright world beneath ;
When at the turn of the winding road,
   Muffled and dark, stood the form of Death !

Life grew cold in the dreary shade ;
   Faded his laughter and ceased his song ;
Over the heavens and across the glade
   Brooding shadows fell, black and long !
Motionless—lost in a maze of fear—
   Life stood and gazed on the ghastly Thing,
Then with a wild cry, lone and drear,
   Sank on the cold earth shuddering.

Death stooped kindly and stilled his moans—
  Bore him away from the baleful spot,
Whilst he murmured in tender tones,
  ' Child of the frail world, fear me not !
Mourn not this earth with its languishing bloom ;
  Grieve not to go from its darkness and strife ;
Beauty is brighter beyond the tomb !
  And death alone leads to perfect life !'

THE DEAD YEAR, 1863.

ANOTHER wave spent on the shore of Time;
  One more pulse of Eternity's great heart;
Another echo of that bell whose chime
  Tolls deeply, ' Dust thou art !'

Another year gone down into the dark,
  Its muffled footsteps silent in their tread,
Yet leaving prints by which our eyes may mark
  Its course toward the dead.

Gone with its joys and woes, delights and fears,
  Its radiant promises and blasted hopes ;
Its beauteous dewdrops changed to burning tears,
  Its tears to pearly drops.

Gone with its storms, its sunshine and its showers,
  Its tearful dawnings and its twilight haze ;
Its woodland melodies, its bees and flowers,
  That tranced the summer days.

Gone with the balmy kisses of its spring;
  Gone with the blood-flush of its faded eves;
Gone with its swallow-flight on glimmering wing
  Gone with its fallen leaves.

Gone, ere the echo of its blustering breath
  Has ceased to sweep across th' affrighted waves;
Gone, when long-looked-for eyes are glazed in
      death,
  Down in their ocean graves.

Gone, while as yet the shouts of strife ascend,
  And war's red fury flames in brethren's eyes—
When with the pure air yells of passion blend,
  And carnage flouts the skies.

Dead year! where is the promise of thy birth?—
  Those splendid streaks which at thy dawn were
      seen?
Have Peace and Truth advanced? and is the
      earth
  Better that thou hast been?

Such gloom is round us that a gleam of light
  Can scarcely through the close-piled shadows
      stray—
And yet I know the darkest hour of night
  Is just before the day!

Then sleep, dead year, among thy kindred dust,—
 Though death and tears have marked thy
     darkened reign,
Though war's wild clamours have been thine—we
     trust
 Thou hast not lived in vain.

And sweep, O Time, along thy silent way,
 Till the last shadow of the Night be gone,
And we behold on the horizon gray
 The laughing light of Dawn !

A NATION'S NEW YEAR'S GIFT.

(January 8, 1864.)

THE New Year landed on Albion's shore,
    And stood where her cliffs rise, shelf o'er shelf;
He greeted the isle with his sunniest smile,
    And thus he kept communing with himself:
'Oh, what shall I give for a New Year's gift
    To these hardy islanders, brave and free,—
My goodwill to prove—to merit their love—
    And make them with gladness remember me?

'I view with sorrow their vacant works;
    I miss the clack of their empty mills;
I see their poor at the workhouse door,
    And I bless the pity that succours and fills!
And my heart bleeds when I turn to gaze
    On the long black shadow that shrouds the
       Throne,
Since the Nation's pride in his manhood died,
    And left the Monarch to mourn alone!

' What can I give that will scatter the gloom,
　　And make the glowings of gladness start ?
That will waken a gleam in eyes that stream,
　　And chase the woe from the mourner's heart ?
I have it !　I have it !　I'll bring, I'll bring,
　　A son and heir to the island's crown !
And I know, oh, I know, every heart will glow
　　With a dear delight which no grief can drown !'

And the Nation takes her new-born Hope,
　　And cradles it in her warm caress—
While her welcomes rise to the echoing skies
　　In a pæan of thrilful tenderness !
O babe of the brilliant destinies !
　　Though thy path through life may all-glorious
　　　　prove—
Though the glitter and shine of all wealth will be
　　thine—
　　Thy greatest wealth is the Nation's love !

APRIL.

Gusty March is dead and gone!
  April heard his parting sighs,
  Smiling through her tearful eyes
At the sweet days coming on.

Nature caught the lustre meek
  From her mild eye twinkling blue;
  Caught and kept the pearly dew
Trickling from her tender cheek.

Young leaves laughed to see her come;
  Drowsy streams began to dance;
  Brooks looked up with grateful glance;
Bees gave forth a happy hum.

Flowers flocked to greet their Queen:
  Daisies peeped out pure and sweet,
  All to kiss her dainty feet
As she tripped across the green.

Swallows twittered 'neath the caves;
    Sweet buds shed their odorous charms;
    Trees stretched forth their naked arms
Praying to be clad with leaves.

Thus—all earth renewed the while—
    Happy April passes by;
    April of the dewy eye!
April of the sunny smile!

Passes on her balmy way—
    With large love and tender care,
    Weaving garlands for the hair
Of her younger sister May!

MOLLY.

(See 'Polly' in *Good Words* for April, 1864.)

Pug nose,
    Red hair,
Short clothes,
    Ankles bare ;

Saucy eyes
    As e'er were seen,
Monstrous size
    Of crinoline.

Bells rung
    Late and soon ;
Songs sung
    Out of tune.

Dust sensations
    In the lobby ;
Flirtations
    With the bobby.

Telling lies—
    Thinks it fun ;
Laughs or cries—
    All's one.

Washing dishes,
    Arms all red ;
Often wishes
    She were wed.

Sunday out,
    Meets Pat ;
Walks about,
    Chit-chat.

Glances sly,
    Talks folly ;
Winks her eye—
    That's Molly.

Goes to bed,
    Falls asleep ;
Through her head
    Visions creep.

Watch her smile
    In fancied blisses,
For a while
    Now she's missis.

Time to rise,
     Heaves a sigh—
From her eyes
     Visions fly.

Gets up
     Dull and fat ;
Breaks a cup,
     Blames the cat.

Half asleep
     Though she be,
Heaven keep
     My maid for me !

And should she wish
     Some worthier poet,
I'll let the bard
     Of ' Polly ' know it.

Then she may live
     In song impearled,
And *Good Words* give
     Her to the world.

SHAKESPEARE.

(Arpil 23, 1864.)

A GLITTERING host of starry-lustred names
    Shine in our England's annals: men who
        wrought
To give us golden truths in fairy frames,
    Or weave the rich-hued thought.

Great-hearted ones, who changed life's common
        things
    To forms of luminous beauty, and gave forth
Their dream-born splendours on bedazzling wings
    To charm the wondering earth:

Investing fleshless phantoms of the brain
    With shapes of radiant immortality,
Or threading tender words in some sweet strain
    To melt men's hearts for aye.

But as the stars, which deep-eyed lustre throw
    When night dreams in the welkin weird and dun,
Grow dim and fade before the full-orbed glow
    Of the uprising sun—

So, at a thought of Shakespeare all the throng
  Of poet-names that make our records bright,
Are blotted from the firmament of song
  By his eclipsing light.

He shines alone in self-created fame—
  No brighter for the burnish we would bring—
Drawing our reverence by the three-fold claim
  Of prophet, priest, and king.

True prophet he! with calm eyes looking forth
  Into the future, and with ears that heard
An echo of the worship of the earth
  In farthest ages stirred!

High-priest in Nature's temple! where the walls
  Are built of leafy branches, and the hush
Of prayer is broken by the clear low calls
  Of linnet, lark, and thrush!

Great king! whose power still sways the minds of
      men,
  Casting o'er all the magic of his might;
Holding the Heaven-dowered sceptre of the pen,
  And ruling by its right.

He wrote for every station, age, and mood ;
  The images and thoughts he lived to weave
Impregnate all our intercourse, and brood
  In every air we breathe.

The offsprings of his fancy are our friends ;
  We clasp their hands at corners of the street ;
And some vague motion of his spirit blends
  With all things that we meet.

'Mong his creations evermore we move.
  We hear Cordelia murmuring sweet and low,
Philosophize with Hamlet, and make love
  With rash-brained Romeo.

In the weird twilight of the woodland glade
  We see his fairies dancing in a ring ;
And where the lone heath lies in baleful shade
  We hear his witches sing.

We muse with Jacques among the forest nooks,
  While Touchstone's bells come tinkling on the
      wind ;
We linger by the boskage and the brooks
  With bright-eyed Rosalind.

We watch rough battle-harnessed warriors rouse
   And blow their trumpets in dim wintry dawns;
We hear Venetian lovers breathe their vows
   On happy moon-lit lawns.

We listen to Prospero's muttered charms,
   Or watch Miranda tripping o'er the green;
We see the Roman dying in the arms
   Of Egypt's swarthy queen.

We hear the hoary Cardinal lament
   His own ambition and his king's disdain;
We see demented Lear with raiment rent,
   And head bared to the rain.

Titania dances lightly through our dreams;
   Puck darts a greeting from arch-gleaming eye:
And Ariel loads the breezes with rich streams
   Of rapturous melody.

We weep for gentle Desdemona's fate:
   We mourn the fatal anguish of belief
That burdened dark Othello with the weight
   'Of an o'erwhelming grief.

We shudder as we watch the murderous Thane
   Creep stealthily to Duncan's chamber door,
Or hear his wife bewail the drops that stain
   Her hand for evermore.

From out some gabled hostel, all the night
　　Pour shouts of drunken mirth, and just before
The cold dawn strikes the world with sudden light
　　Falstaff reels from the door.

On hoofs of clattering fury dashes past
　　The fierce-eyed Hotspur panoplied for war,
While clash of arms and many a bugle blast
　　Ring faintly from afar.

And in all times and places, to our sight
　　Fair forms and old familiar faces rise—
The smile of tenderest friendship, and the light
　　Of laughter-brimming eyes.

The name of Shakespeare is a household word ;
　　It passes from our lips with liquid flow,
And causes at our hearts where'er 'tis heard
　　A freshness and a glow !

And here, there, everywhere—before, behind,
　　Around us and about us evermore—
His spirit broods and hovers, and we find
　　Beauty unfound before !

Great master of all moods that sway the mind !
　　Who poured forth truths all fresh and glittering !
Whose God-like love and tenderness could find
　　Some ' good in everything !'

We cannot speak his praises as we ought;
  Our eyes are dazzled by excess of light:
And on our faltering tongues each feeble thought
  Is frozen by his might!

We can but labour fondly to extend
  His influence o'er every land and clime,
Till with our praises distant voices blend
  Far-heard throughout all time;

And from this little isle, that boasts his birth,
  That nursed his genius, and that holds his
     grave,
Freedom and peace and love across the earth
  Roll like a rolling wave,

That, stretching on and upward, in its spread
  O'erwhelms all evil things before it driven,
Its foot based on the wide world, and its head
  High reaching unto heaven!

A HAUNT OF DREAMLAND.

Through the dim spheres of slumber I was borne
    Upon the wingèd chariot of a vision,
To a fair valley, rich as summer morn,
    With sounds and scents elysian.

Above it dreamed the everlasting blue;
    Its bosom glowed with verdure, green and vernal;
And in the trancèd life of tint and hue
    The summer lurked eternal.

No rude sounds came its slumb'rous peace to mar,
    No hint of labour's loud and stern commotion;
Only, as in a dream, was heard afar
    The low lash of the ocean:

And air was heavy with the hum of bees;
    The crisp stream clattered o'er its polished
        pebbles;
And linnets, lost among thick-foliaged trees,
    Trilled forth their lusty trebles.

Far in the west the ruddy sunset glowed,
  But never left the blood-red verge of heaven ;
And faint but mellow was the blush that flowed
  Through the dim bowers of even.

Oh, what a place, I thought to build a home,
  In this still nook close by the narrow river,
Beneath the eternal sunset, where can come
  No sound of strife for ever !

Here, weary strugglers, sick of earth's alarms,
  Will wend, new stores of rest and strength to
      borrow,
And in the haven of its sheltering arms
  Sad hearts forget their sorrow !

Then did I seek the dwellers in the place,
  And found them gliding in bedazzling bright-
   ness,—
Fair shining forms of most celestial grace,
  And most ethereal lightness.

But when I longed to win their greeting warm,
  They seemed to fade behind a hazy curtain,
And, through the voiceless light, each volant form
  Loomed shadowy and uncertain !

In vain I called with loud and piteous moan ;
  Stately and silent through the air they floated ;
And in the valley I was left alone,
  Unwelcomed and unnoted.

Then, bowed down by this loneliness, I fell,
  And cried, 'Oh give me back earth's lowlier
    meadows !
Better the noisy world, than here to dwell
  Among a host of shadows !

' This solitude oppresses me too much—
  The weary, weary hours will lag fear-laden—
No voice of friend, no thrilling at the touch
  Of some white-handed maiden.

' No old-world sounds will come mine ears to
    bless,
  Save ocean's lash, the stream's lay, and the
    twitter
Of birds among the trees, until excess
  Of sweet is changed to bitter.

' Give me again the great world's healthful
    strife,
  Its surging myriads and its mighty rattle ;
And let me fight the earnest fight of life,
  Or fall in thick of battle !

' For who would in this valley fade and droop—
  Bright as it is with hues of heavenly beauty—
Who could wield falchion in the unflinching
    troop
  Of ever-conquering duty !

' O lordliest life,—though deafened with the din,
  Though ofttimes faltering feebly in the distance
To hold with tyranny and wrong and sin
  A-high and brave resistance !'

With that the cold dawn, glimmering clear and
    sweet,
  Came slowly through its pearly portals breaking :
And surging life and labour thronged to greet
  On all sides my awaking.

And I rejoiced that in all humble works
  There dwells divinity beyond our dreaming ;
And that an everlasting beauty lurks
  In deeds of lowliest seeming !

BABY DIED TO-DAY.

Lay the little limbs out straight ;
　Gently tend the sacred clay ;
Sorrow-shaded is our fate—
　Baby died to-day.

Fold the hands across the breast,
　So, as when he knelt to pray ;
Leave him to his dreamless rest—
　Baby died to-day.

Voice, whose prattling infant-lore
　Was the music of our way,
Now is hushed for evermore—
　Baby died to-day.

Sweet blue eyes, whose sunny gleams
　Made our waking moments gay,
Now can shine but in our dreams—
　Baby died to-day.

'Give his lips your latest kiss ;
Dry your eyes and come away ;
In a happier world than this
Baby lives to-day !'

Still a smile is on his face,
   But it lacks the joyous play
Of the one we used to trace—
   Baby died to-day.

Give his lips your latest kiss;
   Dry your eyes and come away;
In a happier world than this
   Baby lives to-day!

OUR ANGEL-KINDRED.

Far in the glories of a fadeless day,
　　Amid excess of beauty, and the swell
Of rich and everlasting melody,
　　Our angel-kindred dwell.

No care can reach them in their radiant home;
　　No night can trail its terror o'er their skies;
No sin can cast around its baleful gloom;
　　No tears can dim their eyes.

Immortal pleasures crowd the golden hours:
　　Undreamed-of beauty basks on every hand;
And odorous breathings from the lips of flowers
　　Fill all the peaceful land.

And bright forms mingling in the holy mirth
　　Pure white-robed dwellers on the blissful
　　　shore,
Our kindred are,—the loved and lost of earth—
　　The happy ' gone before !'

Among them cherub shapes of childhood glide ;
　　Maidens are there with waving locks of gold ;
And manhood in its glory and its pride,
　　And age no longer old !

And he, the last that left us, whose young
　　　life—
　　By laughing, promise-laden breezes driven—
Disdained to meet the rude world's noisy strife
　　And sought the calm of Heaven.

I dream I see him in his radiant rest,
　　Among his angel-kindred up on high,
And honoured as befits the latest guest
　　They welcome to the sky.

Brethren on ministering missions move,
　　Or guide him where'er Heaven's rich marvels
　　　rise,
And sisters look unutterable love
　　Into his answering eyes.

Ah, blessed spirits in their balmy ease !
　　No cross of earth can ever chafe them now !
For them no more the trembling hands and knees
　　Nor doubt-beclouded brow !

Ours is the darkness ; theirs the boundless day ;
    They drink true life ; we draw the laboured
        breath :
They have eternal sunshine on their way ;
    We have the gloom of death.

Yet, nearing the cold river, I rejoice
    That when I pass its darkness and its roar,
All these will welcome me with heart and voice
    Upon the further shore.

THE FALL OF FOYERS.

I STOOD one morning in summer,
   On the rude peak opposite
Where over the rocky Foyers came down
   The cataract foaming white.

No sigh in the air above me;
   No song in the woods around;
A deathlike silence, broken alone
   By the hollow and deep-mouthed sound

Of water for ever falling,
   And boiling and seething below;
Now lashing the crags in its furious ire,
   Now laving them in its flow.

No change in its deep diapason—
   No pause in its passionate dole—
Plaintive and awful, it found and woke
   An echo within my soul !

Grand in its eloquent beauty—
　Great in its infinite might—
It left its rocky home for my heart,
　Overflowing it quite !

Its splendour flooded my spirit !
　And, though hundreds of miles away,
As plain as I saw it that summer morn,
　I can behold it to-day :

Can lie in the night-time and listen
　To the splash and the dash of the tide,
And can see the boiling caldron smoke
　Down the cavern yawning wide !

For all that we witness of beauty,
　All grandeur melting us most,
Passes into eternal possession,
　And can nevermore be lost !

IN THE AUTUMN.

WHERE are the flowers that blossomed
So fair in the bright days of spring;
Where are the swallows that skimmed o'er the land
So gaily on glimmering wing?

Where are the green leaves that whispered
Such marvellous melody?
And the wandering zephyrs that sighed forth their
soul
In odorous kisses to me?

Where is the friend of my bosom?
Why cometh he not to my cries?
So weary am I for the clasp of his hand!
So faint for the light of his eyes!

Ah! once more the blossoming roses
Their delicate bloom will unfold:
The swallows will skim o'er the sunshiny land
On their glimmering wings as of old:

The trees will stretch upward to heaven
    Their bountiful branches of green ;
And the slumbering zephyrs will waken and sigh
    Their mystical music between :

And the passionate kiss of the summer
    Will thrill to the heart as of yore :
But the friend that walked with me in days that
        are gone
Can never come back to me more !

MIDNIGHT.

All hail! thou dark-browed and majestic Queen!
   I watch thy coming with awe-bated breath;
Thy beauty is a terror! and thy mien
   Is as the mien of death!

And yet I love thee, Midnight, with such love
   As steeps my spirit in a dread delight!
A trembling pleasure thrills me as you move,
   Dark-splendid in my sight!

I worship, whilst I wonder at the glow
   Which shines within thy deep and awful eyes:
I joy to see thy star-gemmed tresses flow
   Across the dusky skies!

I fain would clasp thee to my yearning breast,
   Yet fear thy bosom's cold and clammy touch;
With one wild kiss I'd ease my heart's unrest,
   But dread thy lips too much!

A vague strange passion stirs my inmost soul—
  My whole frame tingles when I feel thee near,
And o'er my heart's mysterious surgings roll
  Tremors of joy and fear !

I marvel, is such beauty, lone and rich,
  Devoid of being and the spirit's gleam ?
Or knows it not some truer life, of which
  Our gross minds may not dream ?

But never falls the answer ; and perforce
  I stand and watch and wonder from afar,
To see thee sweep on thy majestic course
  To meet the morning star !

REQUIESCAT IN PACE.

(1864.)

WE weep our farewell to the parting Year,
   Who totters to his grave so worn and hoary;
'Tis meet that we should drop a tribute tear
   O'er all his vanished glory.

We'll bid a kind adieu, however brief,
   And when he leaves us, sad and weary-hearted,
We'll speak of him in tones of tremulous grief,
   As of a friend departed.

What though his garments have been stained
     with blood,
   And his fast-glazing eyes with wrath been
     lighted;
Though virtue has been trampled on, and good
   Been ofttimes blurred and blighted!

What though red Ruin, in the track of War,
    Has breathed its fiery breath o'er fertile regions,
While all the world stood wondering from afar,
    And watched the battling legions !

What though the hope of years is unfulfilled ;
    Though o'er us angel-joys have ceased to hover,
And many a brave high-beating heart is stilled,
    Its vain life-struggle over !—

We know the Guide of systems and of suns
    In all of this world's government engages,
And trust that an all-perfect purpose runs
    Through all the wildering ages.

Ah, could our blinded stubborn natures learn
    To yield submissively to faith's possessing,
In present seeming ills we might discern
    The germs of future blessing ;

Might trace through all the acts that build the
        years
    The working of some heaven-appointed duty :
Might find in all our sorrows, cares, and fears
    A fitness and a beauty :

And, gazing onward but a little way,
   Might see an earth all glorious, fair, and
      vernal—
Love holding o'er each heart its magic sway,
   And Peace enthroned eternal :

No cloud of sorrow brooding anywhere ;
   No dreaded ill in the dark future folden ;
No sigh save that of the warm summer air
   Wafted on pinions golden !

Then pass away, and rest in peace, Old Year—
   And while a stranger voice takes up thy story,
We needs must drop the tribute of a tear
   O'er all thy gloom and glory.

WHEN YOU ARE FAR AWAY, LOVE.

I STAND upon the sea-washed strand
   And watch the closing day, love,
Where oft we loitered hand in hand
   Before you went away, love.

The waters ripple at my feet,
   They dart up creek and bay, love,
And dimly dimple cold and sweet,
   But you are far away, love.

The home-bound boats, with rounded sails,
   Dance o'er the dancing spray, love,
The merry zephyr flouts and fails,
   But you are far away, love.

The crescent moon creeps up the east
   And wades in vapoury gray, love,
The wild bird's vesper hymn has ceased,
   And you are far away, love.

I miss the warm light of your eye,
Your low voice, soft and gay, love,
And therefore I must heave a sigh
That you are far away, love.

And yet I know where'er thou art
Thy thoughts will hither stray, love,
So there is music in my heart,
Though thou *art* far away, love.

THE BIRDIES.

A WEE bird, weary o' her hame,
    Flew far awa' into the west,
An' whaur she thocht nae birdies came,
    She built hersel' a lanely nest.

A neibor birdie, cauld an' weet,
    Ae day socht shelter i' the tree,
An' near the nestie, low an' sweet,
    He sang his luve fu' tenderly.

She listened wi' a flutterin' breast;
    An' losin' a' her lanely pride,
She bad' him 'till her cosy nest,
    An' creepit closely to his side!

An' aye sinsyne, in weal or woe,
    The birdies hae been ne'er apart;
By day they heavenwards singin' go,
    By nicht they nestle heart to heart.

ABRAHAM LINCOLN.

(Assassinated April 14, 1865.)

THE world stands tearfully and holds its breath,
  Wrapt in a speechless trance of grief and
    wonder
To hear the story of a great man's death
  In mutterings of thunder.

The sad news hushes shouts of party strife;
  No cold disparagement one murmur raises;
And those who were his bitterest foes in life
  Are first to speak his praises.

An honest, fearless, simple-minded man,
  Of purpose firm and earnest high endeavour,
Whose name shall live till history's latest span,
  A talisman for ever.

The foremost spirit in his native land,
  Framing unflinchingly his great life story;
Torn from his toil by a base dastard's hand
  In his mid-hour of glory,

Labouring to strike the shackles from the slave,
　　And build a work whose fame shall be
　　　　eternal :—
Freedom shall lay her chaplet on his grave,
　　And keep it green and vernal.

We think of him and cannot feel resigned—
　　Lost to his vast designs when most they need
　　　　him,
And marvel where his countrymen will find
　　One worthy to succeed him.

THY LOVE.

Thy love shall tune this harsh world's noise,
And make its tangled wastes rejoice;
Shall through the darkness cast its ray
To glorify my lonesome way.

Thy love shall elevate my mind
And make me gentler with my kind;
Shall rule the motions of my blood,
And keep me pure and true and good.

Thy love shall plume my spirit's wings
To soar on high to nobler things;
Shall be my buckler in the strife,
And nerve me for the shocks of life.

Thy love shall be my firmest faith—
Shall even gild the gloom of death,
And through the future worlds 'twill be
The sweetness of eternity!

ON THE BRIDGE.

I STOOD upon a little rustic bridge
  That o'er a narrow bickering brooklet lay,
And watched the sun go down behind a ridge
  Of hillocks far away.

A rosy lustre lived along the skies,
  And isled rich streaks of orange-gloried hue;
While fleecy cloudlets fringed with radiant dyes
  Scudded across the blue.

Eastward a pale moon clomb the azure steep;
  A single star looked forth with quivering glow,
And the brook sent its music, lone and deep,
  Murmurously from below.

The twilight glory melted through my frame;
  The moon held o'er my blood its mystic sway;
The mellow murmur of the brooklet came
  And charmed my heart away!

And ere the sunset faded from the tips
  Of those far hills, some spirit of the eve
Breathed forth a song more sweet than mortal
    lips
  Could frame, or heart conceive !

Still in my soul its low wild echoes live,
  Its sweet, weird measure makes me oft rejoice,
But ah ! strive how I may, I cannot give
  Its wondrous music voice !

PALMERSTON.

Our gray-haired chieftain toiling in the van,
  Who linked his country's present to its past ;
The merry-hearted, marvellous old man
  Is stricken down at last.

'Tis meet that we should mourn him whose firm
    hand,
  Though blanched by eighty winters, still could
    hold
The helm of State, and guide his native land
  'Mid dangers manifold.

His every thought was England's; prompt to
    guard
  The pride and glory of her pure renown ;
Quick to defend her honour ; wise to ward
  All peril from her crown.

His hoary winter seemed to mimic spring,
  And bear the blossoms of the sunny hours;
The freshness of the spirit served to fling
  Its force o'er all his powers.

The cheery voice; the hale and hearty form;
  The friendly faith; the judgment all elate;
The sharp retort; the tact to quell the storm
  Or turbulent debate:

The courage and the constancy; the truth
  And earnestness that underlay the crust
Of outward levity; the heart of youth;
  The fervour and the trust:

The rounded life in which there did not lurk
  One wish that was not for his country's weal;
The vigorous frame that found a joy in work:
  The never-tiring zeal:—

All these in him we grieve for held their part:
  Britannia mourns a great and worthy son,
Since the death-angel stilled the gallant heart,
  And whispered his 'Well done.'

POEMS.

1866—1869.

A WHISPER OF THE SPRING.

Shut out from Nature and each natural thing,
  Within the city's dusty purlieus buried,
I heard to-day a whisper of the spring
  As through the streets I hurried.

A soft low zephyr that had lost its way
  Came, rich with balmy odour from far meadows,
And breathed on dingy piles, that all the day
  Stand frowning o'er their shadows.

All timidly and sweet it crept along:
  A prisoned throstle felt the wafted wonder,
And shrilled a welcome, as if gushing song
  Would tear its throat asunder.

And in a moment I was borne away
  From the great Babel's mighty din and bustle,
To where through woodland glades the soft winds
    play,
  Making the young leaves rustle.

I saw the daisies gemming all the green ;
    The hawthorn blossom peeping from the
        hedges ;
The lazy brooklet purling on between
    Long lines of sleepy sedges.

The dew-drops glistened in the sun-glints fair ;
    The blear-eyed cattle browsed in grassy
        hollows ;
The sheep-bells tinkled clear, and all the air
    Was jubilant with swallows.

The honeysuckle with the sweetbrier wreathed ;
    The waving meadows lay in sunny stretches ;
The wooing air its wanton love-sigh breathed
    Among the early vetches.

And Nature wore so beautiful a dress,
    Across her features such a glory floated,
That I stood in a trance of tenderness,
    And like a lover gloated !

But momentary was the spell ! for soon
    The zephyr's gentle breath was all expended,
And up the dreary street the throstle's tune
    Grew fainter and then ended ;

And died away from me each rapturous sound!
  Faded the landscape with its fresh-born
    beauties!
Leaving me to an uninviting round
  Of dull and prosy duties!

Yet all day long in crowded street or mart,
  Amid the great town's ceaseless stir and jostle,
I felt the sweet breeze play about my heart
  And heard the clear-toned throstle.

GREEN LEAVES.

Sunny Spring is here at last,
    Breathing hints of buds and clover;
Frosts, and snows, and storms are past;
    Winter's dreary reign is over:
Not a thought in Nature grieves,
All things 'babble of green leaves.'

I can hear the zephyr sigh
    O'er the height and through the hollow;
Lark-notes raining from on high,
    Hum of bee and song of swallow:
Idyls that the mavis weaves
In this 'babble of green leaves.'

Shady nook and grassy dell,
    Daisy, crocus, snowdrop, pansy,
Hawthorn blossom, sweet blue-bell,—
    All come crowding on my fancy,
Balmy mornings, blessed eves—
In this 'babble of green leaves.'

FAITH.

Man's power is palsied by his want of faith ;
His strong-winged soul is clogged by unbelief ;
His deeds are dwarfed and lustreless,—and Death
Blots out the record brief.

We count this life a vague delusive dream,
Doubt mingles with each dearly-cherished hope ;
We fear that things are other than they seem
As through the dark we grope.

We toil, and rest, and toil—but do not know
When work will cease and perfect rest begin
We joy and grieve—have happiness and woe—
We triumph and we sin !

We feel the varied seasons, cold or warm,
And yield submissively to Nature's laws :
Are tossed about of tempest—drenched by
storm—
But never know the cause !

But had we pure and perfect faith, to take
    All truth into our hearts confidingly,
We might move mountains from their place, and
        break
    The barriers of the sea !

Man's will would prove itself omnipotent,
    Our grovelling souls would from the dust be
        freed,
And Nature, at our feet all lowly bent,
    Proclaim us Gods indeed !

THE LOVERS.

AN IDYL OF THE WAR.

THE Lady Constance loved Sir Lionel
With all the warmth and fervour of first love;
And the young Baron prized her favour more
Than the hot life-blood pulsing in his heart.
She was the only daughter of an Earl;
And he the orphan of her father's friend—
Brought by her father, at his orphanage,
To dwell with him within the vast old Hall
And be a playmate to his little girl.
And they had grown together, like two flowers
That, hidden in a leafy solitude,
Together drink the sunshine and the dews,
And watch each other's beauty glow and grow
Till Spring's fresh days give place to Summer's
     prime.
And ever as their golden youth flew by
The lady loved her lover more and more:
Her every thought, unknown unto herself,

Borrowed its hues from him, and all her life
Became a yearning to possess his heart
And flood his way with beauty and with joy!
But Lionel mourned his own unworthiness,
And mused, 'If I could only do some deed
Of lofty import or triumphant good,
To prove I prize her love beyond all else
Within this breathing Universe of God's,
Then would I glory to heap on her head
The grateful tribute of the world's applause,
And throne her on the topmost peak of Fame.
Resolves will wither 'mong these tranquil ways;
And in this lassitude my nerves will rust.
I must go forth and grapple with the world.'
But evermore upon his musings rose
The vision of a face so pale and meek,
And beautiful in its ethereal peace,
Softening his heart and making him like one
Who, journeying through a strange and unknown
　　　　land,
Lights on two paths and knows not which to take.

So the days crowded past like happy dreams—
When suddenly a noise of war arose,
And England sent her armies o'er the sea
To fight her battles and uphold her rights.
Then Lionel felt an ardour and a zeal,

Drawn from a line of warlike ancestry,
Quicken and spring to life within his soul,
To go forth with the legions of his land
And meet her foes in the wild crash of war.

Sir Lionel nursed this yearning in his heart,
Till, on a summer evening, when the twain
Walked down the mile-long avenue of elms
Before the Hall, and came upon the sea
Basking in moon-lit peace.   Then Lionel said,
' O Constance, I have something on my mind
Which I am sure will cause you grief and pain,
Yet must I speak and tell you what it is.'
She lifted unto him a startled glance,
And gazed a moment in his troubled eyes :
Then, like a bird that seeks its sheltering nest,
Crept to his bosom and this answer made :
' Say on, my Lionel, and be not afraid
To tell me all the trouble in your heart ;
Thy Constance fears not any threatened ill
So she can lay her head on this dear breast
And feel that thou art near her evermore.'
Then he : ' Ah ! therein lies the bitterness
Which makes the strife 'twixt love and duty sore.
Constance, my love has been a happy one,
And happy might I still be, could I stay
To roam with you about our childhood's haunts—

The woods, the cliffs, the streamlets, and the
      hills—
To ride, walk, read with you, and with you tend
The sweet familiar flowers we love so well.
But now I feel I am a boy no more,
And other sterner things put forth their claims
Upon my manhood. I am not so young
That I should stand with women and with babes
And watch the busy workers pressing on
To win the fame that waits on noble deeds,
And never wish to join them in the race,
And struggle forward till I reach the goal!
Many as young as I, with tongue, pen, sword,
Toil in their country's cause, and help along
The freedom and the welfare of the world.
No charms for me have hustings, senates, courts:
My father was a soldier; and I feel
The spirit of my father moves me on
To join the glorious chivalry of war,
And wield a true sword in a holy cause.
I therefore purpose shortly to set forth
Across the seas to fight my country's foes,
And do what one man can to crush their power.'

Constance stood mute and listened to the end;
But when she heard him speaking calmly thus,
And knew that they must part, and that perchance

She ne'er might see his face again, she felt
Like the poor traveller in the sandy waste
Who, with tired footsteps and with parchèd
    tongue,
Draws near the spot toward which he long hath
    toiled
And sees the mirage melting into nought.
But Lionel spake of hope and comfort to her,
And of a future crowned with happiness
When he should take her to his heart, and they
Should feel the pure high bliss of hopes fulfilled
And duties nobly done. Then courage came;
And all the clamorous voices of her heart
Grew quiet as a linnet's callow brood
Fed by the parent bird. She stood erect,
And all the proud blood of her haughty race
Flushed her fair cheeks and mounted to her brow
Like sunrise creeping o'er the pallid dawn.

' Forgive the selfish petulance,' she said,
' Which for a while spread havoc 'mong my
    thoughts
And made my love so little worthy thine.
'Tis past: and now I do not bid thee stay
To waste the golden promise of thy youth
Longer among these scenes of tranquil rest.
Go forth and smite the haters of thy land.

Well know I that 'tis nobler far to heed
The calls of duty than the voice of love.
My love go with thee o'er the stormy seas,
And be thy buckler on the fields of war.
Though but a simple peaceful English maid,
Some touch of Spartan valour in my veins
Gives me the power to say unto thee—" Go."
God shield thee with His arm from ills and death,
And send thee safely home to me again :
But even should my darkest fears prove true,
And thy dear form should fail from off the earth,
Still proudly would I walk the waste of life
In the dimmed lustre of thy love removed,
Knowing that neither death nor absence can
Destroy that love within us, or prevent
Its full fruition in a purer world.'

She ceased ; and both stood silent, gazing o'er
The moon-lit calm of ocean's waveless plain,
Which, in its constant ripple on the shore,
Seemed ever framing low-voiced calls for each
To leave the peaceful dreamland of their youth
And learn to toil and suffer in the world.

Then homeward, silent still, but with full hearts
That spoke a low love-language each to each,

They passed beneath the whispering elms that
    threw
A shadowy tapestry about their path.

So ere the languid moon had thrice turned round
Full-faced to gaze upon the dreaming world,
Lionel departed for the seat of war.
Constance stood on the shore, full wistfully
Watching the white-fledged messenger of fate,
Freighted with all her hopes, sail far away,
Till, on the horizon, like a sea-bird's wing
It gleamed, and dipped into the veiling gray.
Then as she turned she heard within her heart
A whisper like the echo of a bell
That tolls the passing of a soul from earth !
But bravely did she struggle with her grief :
And oftentimes she heard, or deemed she heard,
Low voices murmuring softly in her ear,
' Labour and strive to merit all his love !'
Thoughts of the toilsome life Lionel had chosen—
Its dangers and discomforts—made her own
Seem altogether purposeless and vain :
Whilst out of sorrow for his absence sprang
The wish to minister to others' woes.
No longer did she pass the listless hours
In dreamful lassitude or languid ease,
But all the tenor of her days was changed :

She clothed the wretched, gave the hungry food,
Relieved the suffering, comforted the lorn,
And entered, like a sunbeam, lowly doors,
Gladdening all hearts, and bearing with her thence
A blessing richer than the gifts she brought.

Meanwhile the war was raging far away,
And Lionel, with all ardour, plunged among
The fiery whirl and rush of combatants,
Fleshing right manfully his virgin sword.
Men marvelled at the might of his young arm,
And hailed him as a leader yet to be.
Promotion waited him on every field,
And honours rained upon him thick and fast ;
Till o'er the length and breadth of his own land
His name was bruited as the type and stamp
Of all things noble, chivalrous, and brave.
Constance heard proudly of his growing fame,
And in sweet day-dreams welcomed back again
Her hero-lover to the faithful heart
That yearned to be the pillow of his rest !

So two years passed ; and Lionel had become
A bronzed and bearded chief: his face was seamed
       With many a scar ; and furrowed was his brow
With lines which anxious thought had printed
       there.

Still from beneath stern brow and burnished helm
Looked as of old the frank and fearless eyes,—
That even a child's small hand had trustfully
Sought the hard palm so used to scatter death!

It chanced one night a fortress of the foe
Had to be stormed; and Lionel was chosen
To lead a column up to the assault.
All silently the men moved through the gloom,
Approached the frowning walls, and planting
        there .
The scaling-ladders, with a sudden shout
Dashed o'er the summit like a whelming wave.
But as a wave that climbs a craggy shelf
Is broken and driven back, and leaves behind
Its scattered crust of foam upon the top—
So, soon o'er-mastered by the enemy,
The British troops were beaten from the hold,
Leaving the beetling ramparts strewn with dead.
Again they formed and rallied, with such force
As made the stubborn foe yield step by step;
And Lionel, hovering about the van,
Cheered on his men with words of high
        emprise
And deeds of wondrous prowess, till at length
The enemy was hurled across the heights,
And o'er the turrets England's ensign flapped

With ghostly flutter through the murky night.
Then in that rapturous moment of success,
While yet the youthful leader held on high
His reeking blade, and shouted—' Victory,'
A bullet hissing through the folded smoke
Shattered his sword arm, and he reeled and fell.

His comrades bore him sadly from the place :
And, faint with suffering and loss of blood,
For weary days he lay like one o'er whom
Life and Death struggle for the masterdom.
Still he revived ; but with a shattered frame,
Wasted and weakened by his wound, and worn
By long exposure to the heat and cold,
And toiling in the trenches night and day ;
So, that ere duty he could well resume,
A fever that was raging in the camp
Seized on him and prostrated him anew.
Then often in his blank deliriousness
He raved of olden things—his boyhood's days—
The dog he hunted with—the horse he rode—
The grim Hall hid among the shadowy elms—
The brook that flashed its dimples in the sun—
The cliffs that looked bare - breasted o'er the
    main—
The restless heaving sea, that evermore
Whispered its drowsy secrets to the strand :

And with all these was mingled that one name
Whose gentle influence lulled the stormy soul
And beautified delirium's hideous dreams.
Oft, too, his spirit moved 'mid war's alarms;
He yelled aloud his furious battle-cries,
Shrieked forth defiance, and his rolling eyes
Were full of the wild frenzy of the fight.

Three weeks the fever lasted : and at length—
When reason dawning in the wildered brain
Left the racked body like a stranded wreck
Cast on a dreary barren shore, and lost
To use and strength and purpose in the world—
Lionel prayed, 'Let me see, before I die,
Constance and England, and I die in peace.'
Then they who watched him said among them-
    selves,
' Right nobly has he lived and fought and bled ;
Why should we cross his lightest wish in death ?'
And so they bore him to a home-bound ship,
Bade him farewell, and as he sailed away,
They shook their heads and muttered, 'All too late !
He ne'er will look on England's shores again !'

But will and yearning gave his body strength,
And confidence inspired the sick man's hope.
Oft in the dreamy noontide heat he lay
Upon his pallet on the vessel's poop,

And watched as in a waking dream the curved
And changeful pathway on the pathless deep.
But thought and fancy wandered otherwhere—
To England's shores, and to another home
He knew he was approaching day by day.

And Constance daily watched for his return:
But with how changed a feeling from the joy
With which, in bygone days, she had foretold
Her warrior-love's triumphant welcome home.
Still all the memory of his nobleness,
The glory and the fame that he had won,
His love of country, and his scorn of death,
Came o'er her sad heart like a morning song,
And almost changed her sorrow into joy.
'And why,' she thought, 'should we not welcome
      him
With honour and rejoicing, as a chief
Whose faith and valour have not been in vain?'
So when at last he reached his native shore,
The Hall was dressed as for a festival;
Porches and pillars were festooned with flowers:
Triumphant arches rose along the way
With 'Welcome,' and with 'Honour to the brave;'
And through the surging, cheering crowds they
      brought
The dying soldier like a victor home.

'And then, by virtue of her wifehood, moved
About his couch in gentle offices
Of tender ministration and fond care.

Then, on the morrow, Constance decked herself
In pearls and glistening raiment like a bride,
And seeking Lionel's chamber, with a priest,
They two were bound, at her most earnest wish,
In wedlock's holy and most sacred bonds.
The ceremony over, she arose,
And laid aside her gems and glittering robes,
And then, by virtue of her wifehood, moved
About his couch in gentle offices
Of tender ministration and fond care.
But ere a week had passed, one eventide—
When the low sun looked through the leafy elms
And filled the chamber with a mystic glow—
The faint head clasped within the faithful arms
Sank feebly on the pillow, while a smile
Broke o'er the features, and the tired soul
Passed to where all the weary shall have rest.

And so the virgin-wife put on the weeds
Of widowhood, and for three lonely years—
In sorrow for her love's untimely fate,
In pride to bear his dear and honoured name,
In almsgiving, and in acts of charity—
She lived, and then Death sought her like a friend
She wished not for, but welcomed when he came.

AUTUMN.

Summer has gone, and, like a new-made wife,
The shade of household cares upon her brow,
Autumn has come, clad in a russet cloak,
With winds that wither all the summer flowers,
With ripening grain and fruits and falling leaves.

The sun has lost half of his summer heat;
The morns and eves are windy, drear, and cold,
The round full moon looks blushingly on earth;
And blasts come howling from the barren moors
That scatter o'er the land the fallen leaves.

And when the Autumn will lie down and die
Upon the lap of Winter, his last look
Will fall on trees that lift their naked arms
To the dark skies, and his dark breath will move
Along the lanes, and fan the fallen leaves.

Life has its autumn, cold and bleak, when hopes
Long nourished by the sunshine of romance
Wither and fall, too burdensome to bear;
Then feel we life's long winter drawing nigh,
And read man's history in the fallen leaves.

A CHRISTMAS SONG.

A SONG of the merry Christmas-time,
    Let each from the heart forth fling.
Come, banish all sadness, and join with all glad-
      ness,
    To welcome the rare old King ;
    And merrily, cheerily, .
Uplift all your voices and sing.

Ring out, O bells, with your musical chime,
    Clatter and hammer and swing,
Till dull ears are shaken and echoes all waken,
    To welcome the jovial King ;
    While merrily, cheerily,
We lift up our voices and sing.

Voices and hearts from each far-distant clime
    Shall homage and fealty bring ;
From land and from ocean, loud cries of devotion
    Will welcome the blithe old King ;
    As merrily, cheerily,
We lift up our voices and sing.

THE OLD YEAR, 1866.

THE old year is almost dead ;
  He is feeble and withered and gray ;
We gather around his death-bed,
  And watch him passing away:
We think of the ill he has wrought—
We speak of the good he has brought—
And Memory her action is plying,
As the old year lies a-dying.

Tempest and havoc and death,
  Murrain and shipwreck and grief;
Pestilence with its poisonous breath ;
  Battle bloody, though brief:
Kings of their crowns have been bereft,
Widows and orphans sorrowful left,
And the sounds of sadness and sighing
Greet the old year while a-dying.

But our thoughts are not all sad:
  Freedom now claims for her own
Glorious regions where long her glad
  Fair presence has been unknown.

The Old Year, 1866.

Error is tottering on her throne,
Hemispheres have been linked in one,
Words of peace 'neath ocean are flying
As the old year lies a-dying.

We bid the old year good-bye ;
   We welcome blessing and ban,
As the lessons sent from on high
   Teaching his duties to man.
Oh, may we gird us for the fight,
And in the cause of Truth and right
Let us be found together vying
As year after year lies a-dying !

THE CUCKOO.

I HEARD the cuckoo at the evening's close
   Trill its low calls from out a bower of blossom,
And, at the sound, a thrill of joy arose
   And trembled through my bosom.

A sudden rapture lived in every vein;
   My heart leaped up to greet the glad new-comer;
And dreams of childhood danced about my brain
   In whispers of the summer!

Could I translate that thrill of joy to men—
   To weary struggling souls could I but show it
In sweetness and in tenderness—ah, then
   I might be deemed a poet!

THOU ART THE LODE-STAR OF MY LIFE.

Thou art the lode-star of my life,
  My warmest wishes turn to thee;
Through all this dim world's dust and strife
  Thy lustre calmly beams on me!

Thou art the sweetest flower that sheds
  Its fragrance on my dreary way;
From thee springs all the joy that spreads
  Around my path from day to day!

Ah! I would toil both soon and late,
  Would scale this rough world's thorny steep,
And many a weary year I'd wait,
  And many a wakeful vigil keep;—

Happy, if, when the turmoil past,
  A haven smiled of peaceful rest,—
I found the radiant star at last,
  I wore the flower upon my breast!

OUR LOST ONE.

We lost our darling years ago,
　But have not ceased to mourn him yet:
We ever speak of him in low
　And tender tones of deep regret:
Old places bring his image near;
　Old pleasures speak to us of him;
　Old playthings make our eyes grow dim
With memories sorrowful and dear!

We gather round the fire by night,
　And tell the tales of long ago;
And in the weird and ruddy light
　We watch each other's features glow:
We sing some gay and jovial air;
　Our laughter shakes the echoing walls;
　But o'er our hearth for ever falls
The shadow of his vacant chair!

And if by chance someone should wake
　A merry strain he may have sung,—
Or if his whispered name should break
　In trembling utterance from the tongue;—

A moisture gathers in our eyes ;
  A hush falls on us from above ;
  And to the yearnings of our love
Again we see his image rise !

We see again the golden hue
  Of sunny tresses waving free !
We see from eyes of deepest blue
  Long lashes lifted wonderingly !
Gay noises from old corners start ;
  Low laughter ringing clear and sweet,
  And patterings of little feet
Waken old echoes in the heart !

Poor grovellers still among the dust,
  We cannot lift our souls on high,
In purest faith and perfect trust,
  To thee, our lost one, in the sky !
Still earth's delusive hopes we chase ;
  Its vain imperfect pleasures quaff;
  Half of our love is here, but half
Must reach thee in thy radiant place !

Oh, far beyond our earth-bleared ken,
  In concourse of the good and wise,
Dost thou not view the ways of men
  And all their littleness despise ?

With wonder in thy downward glance
    Dost thou behold our actions here?—
    Ah, pity thou our guilt and fear,
Our frailty and our ignorance!

When weary of the toilsome road,
    Besprinkled with the dust of care,
Bowed down beneath the weighty load
    Of burdens that we still must bear!
Wondering when all this toil shall cease!
    Yearning to win the promised rest!
    Stoop from thy home among the blest
With breathings pure of heavenly peace!

Still hover near us on our way;
    Surround us with thine unseen love;
Restrain us when we seek to stray,
    And gently raise our hopes above!
And when at last the heavenly land
    Shall on our dazzled vision burst,
    O angel-brother, be the first
To stretch to us a welcome hand!

SABBATH CALM.

Lapt in a dream of peace the Sabbath lay,
　　The sunshine playing on its placid breast ;
All nature seemed to know the sacred day,
　　And hush its hoarse unrest.

The trees basked moveless in the sunny glow,
　　The birds skimmed silent through the breezeless
　　　　air ;
The very surge's murmur was as low
　　As is a whispered prayer.

So placid hung the blue sky stretched above,
　　So peaceful lay the bright earth spread below ;
So gentle was the water's waveless move,
　　So faint and hushed its flow ;—

That I, o'erwearied with this rude world's
　　　　storms,—
　　By clamorous week-day tempests tossed and
　　　　driven,—
Could almost deem I breathed the air that forms
　　The eternal calm of heaven !

TO A CAGED NIGHTINGALE.

Is it for joy thou pourest forth thy heart
  In a rich flood of music, loud and long ?
If so, what means the plaint that forms a part
  Of such triumphant song ?

What blessedness has made thy spirit glad ?
  What unknown grief can in thy breast be
    bound ?
Ah, sorrow sure did never ring so sad !
  Nor joy more joyful sound !

But thine is not the only breast on earth
  Where clash the two extremes of joy and
    grief !—
Nor lone heart to whom pleasure's wildest mirth
  Can bring but poor relief !.

Thou long'st to revel in the free sunshine,
  Or nestle in some grove where green leaves
    play :—
And so this weary prisoned soul of mine,
  Like thee, would fly away !

ROSE.

On the margin of the woodland, hidden half by
    leafy shadows,
  There stands a little cottage, ivy-clad and rose-
    embowered;
Before it stretches far and wide a wealth of
    waving meadows,
  Behind it lies the forest with a slumbrous
    dark endowered.

Here, in the sunny days of Spring, from out
    among the bushes,
  Spring-flowers peep on passers-by with bright
    eyes all aglow;
And through the gloaming's breathless reign the
    nightingale in gushes
  Pours forth its plaintive melody all passionate
    and low.

But it is not the tender flowers that tempt my feet
　　to wander
　Down to that cottage through the weird and
　　lonely light of even,
Nor are those notes the nightingale's that make
　　me pause and ponder—
　Is that wild strain a song of earth or music sent
　　from heaven ?

Ah, Rose! the rose blooms on your cheek, your
　　bright eyes gleam and glisten,
　As standing 'mong the dewy flowers you carol
　　clear and wild ;
What can an old man do but stand and strain his
　　ear to listen,
　Till all his heart is flooded and his senses are
　　beguiled ?

Strange that a voice has so much power ! and yet
　　its thrilling sweetness
　Awakes a slumbering echo of the old delightful
　　days,
When all the warm blood through my veins
　　coursed with a feverish fleetness,
　And Youth and Hope lit up the world with
　　their bewitching rays.

Again I seem the careless boy before whose
    raptured vision
  The Future stretched in glittering and iris-
    gloried gleams,
And all the beckoning earth was bathed in light
    that seemed elysian—
  A light that clothed my waking thoughts and
    coloured all my dreams.

Again I hear the solemn forest startled with the
    laughter
  Of happy boys and maidens at their picnic
    'neath the trees ;
Till all its echoes rouse from sleep, and strange
    and hoarsely after
  Give forth their ghostly murmurings upon the
    passing breeze.

Again I wander through the woods or down beside
    the river
  To nurse mysterious yearnings, and to muse on
    many things ;
To watch the dewy leaflets in the sunshine dance
    and quiver,
  Or see the sailing swallows skimming on their
    dusky wings

Again a soft hand seeks mine own, and in its
    trustful clasping
  I count a greater wealth than all the riches of
    a throne !—
So small and soft !—it seems to melt within my
    ruder grasping,
  And yet its slightest touch hath power to thrill
    me to the bone !

Again we tread the forest-paths while curious
    leaves are peering,
  To catch a glimpse of her sweet face ere light
    and shadow part :
Hand locked in hand we pass along in silent bliss,
    each fearing
  To break with spoken words upon the whisper-
    ings of the heart !

Again I see her standing where her garden roses
    blossom—
  The flow'rets listening to her as she carols all
    alone ;
And I think, 'When shall I wear thee, O my
    rosebud, on my bosom ?
  Oh, when shall all thy fragrance and thy beauty
    be mine own ?'

'Again I see her standing where her garden roses blossom—
The flow'rets listening to her as she carols all alone.'

'Mine own!' and yet I sometimes deemed the
thought a wild presumption,
Would plead my dull unworthiness and press
her to forget,—
Until a shower of sunny sparkles chased the mad
assumption
From wonder-widened eyes that shone 'neath
lashes long and wet!

Alas! for all the darling dreams I cherished with
a holy
And tender joy! they seemed not made to
melt and pass away!
Alas! for all the hopes that died and left me
crushed and lowly,
To weep in wasting anguish o'er their pre-
mature decay!

'Tis long ago, and yet my heart will evermore
remember
The sad and desolate day that was my darling's
last on earth,
When all the mellow beauties of the many-hued
September
Seemed frowning as the Winter frowns amid his
dreary dearth!

From early, early morning I had lingered by her
　　dwelling,
　　But ere the ruthless day had reached its brazen
　　　　noon—she died!
Then I rose up, my brain on fire, my breast with
　　tempest swelling,
　　And wandered, stunned and tearless, through
　　　　the woodlands vast and wide.

Instinctively my footsteps sought a spot where oft
　　together
　　We rested in the shelter of the shadows cool
　　　　and deep,
And there I lay me down and hid my face among
　　the heather,
　　And prayed my heart might melt in tears,—but
　　　　no, I could not weep!

The air was chilly when I rose, and evening's
　　dews were falling,
　　The parting sun poured streams of light be-
　　　　tween the level boles;
And up among the dark tree-tops the callow
　　rooks were calling,
　　Their ghostly wailings sounding like the
　　　　shrieks of prisoned souls.

I hastened from the forest, for a sickening dread
    came o'er me,
  And sent a shiver through my frame,—a cold
    sweat to my brow;
I held my breath for very fear, 'till calm and still
    before me
  I saw the village lie, and stood where I am
    standing now.

It was an evening such as this; the rosy light
    was streaming
  On many objects, but it left *her* cottage in the
    shade;
While halfway up the eastern slope the yellow
    moon lay dreaming,
  And faint sounds floated up from where the
    village children played.

The place is little changed since then, but, ah!
    how changed the feeling
  From that with which I stood and gazed upon
    my crushing grief!
For then the fount of woe within my breast
    seemed all congealing,
  But now a flood of tears can come and bring
    my heart relief.

Long years have followed that sad day, and yet
        through all their changes
   Each spot about the village with her spirit
        seems imbued ;
I feel her warm breath on my cheek in each faint
        breeze that ranges,
   I hear her voice in each low sound that stirs the
        solemn wood !

And standing here without the hedge while
        maiden Rose is singing,
   The lingering sunbeams pouring on her head
        their golden blaze,
Within my heart the magic bells of memory are
        ringing,
   With a sweet sadness in their swell, the chimes
        of olden days !

Ah ! other hands are busy 'mong the flowers *she*
        loved so dearly,
   And other feet trip lightly down the little
        garden pad !
Where she once sang another voice is warbling
        wild and clearly !
   Another Rose blooms where she bloomed ! yet
        now I am not sad !

The village church lies basking in the waning
    light of even,
  I know the glow is fading now from chancel
    and from nave;
The tall spire points where she has gone,—up to
    yon gloaming heaven,
  And I grieve not that its shadow lengthens o'er
    her quiet grave!

Nor do I mourn my dreary life with all its lone
    dejection,
  Its lack of sympathy,—its lost delights,—its
    homeless hearth;
Since these have only served to lift on high the
    soul's affection,
  And teach the heart to build its love-nest some-
    where far from earth.

Still, often in the twilight, I can feel a Presence
    near me,—
  Can hear the well-belovèd accents whisper as of
    yore!
I start,—'tis but a dream!—yet even dreams have
    power to cheer me,
  And I muse and muse upon it till the vision
    comes once more!

Am I growing mad ? I know not.   Am I wearing
    near my dotage ?
  I cannot tell ;—but oft the fancy makes my
    heart rejoice,
That her bright spirit hovers round the dear old
    ivied cottage,
  And that the twilight songs are echoed by no
    earthly voice !

And so each day at eventide when pale stars dusk
    and glimmer
  Like angel-eyes that strive to pierce through
    heaven's all-placid blue,
And light wanes in the western sky, and earth
    grows dim and dimmer,
  And wanton wild-flowers drop asleep all
    drunken with the dew,—

I wander by the forest-skirts and feel her white
    hands flinging
  Sweet thoughts of comfort o'er my soul to
    soothe its lonely care,
While, ever and anon, there comes the fairy music
    ringing
  In sweeps of passionate plaintiveness upon the
    eddying air !

And strange thoughts struggle at my heart when-
    e'er I stand and hear it ;
  In vain I peer into the gloom,—no glowing
    form is there !
But I know this body will not long beclog my
    straining spirit,
  That yearns to fly and meet her in the sunny
    realms of air !

Sweep on, O barren Day, and bring the hours
    that will be sweeter !
  Turn on your dusky wheels and pass from the
    dim heavens, O Night !
Hasten the moments rich in bliss when I shall
    spring to meet her,
  And all my darkened life shall merge in ever-
    lasting light !

THE PAST—AND FUTURE.

My life till now has been one varied scene
   Of sunshine and of shade—of joy and grief;
   The years have stolen on me like a thief;
I have well-nigh forgot what I have been!

What have I been? The past let me recall;
   Let all my bygone years before me pass,
   And let me see them all as in a glass
Reflected: let me gaze upon them all.

I've been a child, and tasted all the joy
   That comes in childhood's short-lived summer
      day;
   I've felt those thoughts for ever passed away,
The venturous visions of the dreaming boy.

Sweet are the joys of childhood: sweeter still
   The thoughts that come in dreamy days of
      youth,
   Ere yet the world has lost its look of truth,
Ere yet we sin with judgment and with will.

I've been a lover, and beneath the trees
    On moonlit nights have whispered words of
        love,
    While all the stars looked brightly from above,
And all around was peace; the fragrant
        breeze

Played softly on the lovely cheek of her
    Who sat beside me, beautiful and fair,
    And lifted up her wealth of silvery hair,
And shook the branches with a gentle stir

Like music. Sweet it was on nights like this
    To sit beside her, clasping her soft hand;
    To feel the thoughts I scarce could understand,
Those strange, tumultuous throbs of joys and bliss.

But love, alas! is not all sweet and fair,
    For grief must ever follow in its train;
    It brings us sorrow, and it brings us pain,
And pangs of doubt and moanings of despair.

And I have felt the bitterness at noon—
    The fever raging in my burning head,
    And tossed at midnight on my sleepless bed,
And wept in anguish, while the waning moon

Looked in upon me with its pale, cold beam,
  And seemed to mock me through the long lone
      night
  Till morning came, bringing with it delight
For many ; but, alas ! it brought no gleam

Of joy for me.   'Tis sad that love, sweet love,
  Should glow and radiate in one heart alone,
  And leave another cold and dead as stone—
So stern, so chilly, and so hard to move.

I've been a mourner, and have stood beside
  The bed of suffering, and have held my breath
  To see thee come, O grim destroyer, Death,
And take away with thee our houschold's pride.

Oh, can I e'er forget the tears I shed ?
  Can I forget thy look ?   It haunts me now
  Thy calm and quiet smile, thy glassy brow :
I could not think that thou indeed wert dead.

Yet thou wert dead ; sweetly the Sabbath chimes
  Were sounding when thy spirit passed away,
  As if to bear thee up to realms of day
Upon their swell with joy.   And yet sometimes,

When Vesper draws his curtain round my head,
  And evening settles down serene and gray,
  And care is flitting with the flitting day,
Sometimes I think my brother is not dead.

Thou art not dead ! but only gone before ;
   And in this weary world of sin and pain
   Though we may never see thy face again,
We'll meet thee on that undiscovered shore—

Where thou art gone to dwell midst love and light,
   And joy of which ne'er mortal man did dream ;
   Where truth flows ever onward like a stream,
Where there are no more tears, no death, no
      night.

O, Friendship, how my heart has clung to thee !
   'Mid summer sunshine and 'mid winter's storm
. Still have I seen thy dear familiar form,
Still heard thy fond voice whispering to me.

And yet I have lost many friends ! the waves
   Of time have come and swept them from my
      view :
   Some wander far away, some are untrue,
And some are sleeping in their silent graves.

Wilt thou, my Friend, be but a friend in name,
   And one day realize my darkest fears,
   And change like others with the changing years ?
Or wilt thou be unchangeably the same

As when I knew thee in the first fair days,
    When you and I were blithe and gay and
        young—
    When o'er the fields our happy voices rung
In chorus, and all nature seemed a blaze

Of living glory? But shouldst thou forget,
    Sometimes when Memory holds her silent reign,
    The old times will come back to thee again,
And thou wilt look upon them with regret ;—

Perhaps a thought of me will intervene,
    And thou wilt pause and sadly wonder why
    You feel a tear-drop starting to the eye,
When you review the days that once have been.

And then will come the thoughts of long ago,
    And how together on the summer eves
    We lay beneath the ever-rustling leaves,
And heard the gladsome brooklet's prattling flow ;

Or how upon the dreamy rock-bound shore,
    On softly sweet and beauteous moonlit nights,
    When heaven had hung out all its starry lights,
We sat and heard the deep-mouthed river's roar ;

Or how we felt the full-moon's glorious beam
    Look deeply down from the blue vault above ;
    Or how we dreamed the long sweet dream of
        Love,
Ere yet we knew it was indeed a dream.

And thou wilt think amid the care and strife
    Of this stern world, when that thy heart is sick,
    And fears and troubles sting thee to the quick,
' That was the happiest period of my life.'

Forgive me, O my Friend, my want of faith ;
    Sometimes into my heart such doubts will steal—
    They are but passing shadows, and I feel,
Whate'er betide, that we are friends till death ;

That nought can change thee, nothing e'er destroy
    The band that knits thy soul to mine, my friend ;
    But thou wilt be the same, e'en to the end,
Through days of darkness and through hours of joy.

Oh, let us ever keep our hearts as pure
    And holy as they were in days of youth,
    And let us ever, ever love the truth,
So we may rest in peace—for heaven is sure.

My life indeed has been one varied scene
    Of sunshine and of shade, of joy and grief :
    The years have stolen on me like a thief ;
And I have nigh forgot what I have been !

My joys are sent to cheer me on the road—
  The snare-abounding, rugged road of life;
  My griefs are sent to fit me for its strife;
And both are sent to lead me nearer God—

That God who smiles in sunshine and in shower,
  Who is the Centre of the universe;
  Whose mighty acts no mortal can rehearse,
Or tell His love, or show forth all His power!

I wonder what my future life will be:
  Will it be one of sunshine and of joy?
  Or will I, like a mean and worthless toy,
Be made the sport of fortune's stormy sea?

Sometimes I sit alone in dreary mood,
  And sombre thoughts and vague wild fancies
      come,
  And enter in, and make their darkling home
Within my heart, and then I see no good

In this vain life; what is it but a dream—
  A troubled dream that soon comes to a close,
  Where hopes and fears and griefs and joys and
      woes
Make up for ever its unchanging theme?

I look to the beginning : like a barque
  By prosperous breezes safely borne along,
  Its course doth seem all sunshine and all song ;
I look towards the end, and all is dark.

In vain we seek to pierce the shadowy gloom
  That hides the unknown future from our view ;
  In vain our eyes may strive to struggle through
The veil that hangs behind the silent tomb.

And yet sometimes I sicken 'mid the strife,
  And then those feelings flash across my brain,
  And then those longings come to me again :
' Oh, would that I could know my future life !'

Will I pass onward through this world unknown ?
  Will loves dry up like shallow summer streams ?
  Will hopes fade from me like forgotten dreams,
And leave me in this wilderness alone ?

Or will a few fond hearts still cling to mine,
  Through chance and change, 'mid pleasure or
      distress,
  And twine round me in hours of loneliness,
E'en as the ivy doth round ruins twine ?

Or will I reach the topmost tower of fame,
  And gain a people's lasting gratitude,
  And rank among the great, the wise, the good,
And future generations know my name ?

What maiden shall I clasp unto my breast,
   To be my second self, my dearer life,
   My soft beguiler, comforter, and wife—
My guardian angel till I'm laid at rest?

When will I die?   In life's gay happy prime,
   Ere yet my heart has felt the weight of tears,
   When like a glory burst the future years,
And rainbow-colours tint the coming time?

Or will I linger on to faint old age,
   When worldly cares and tumults all shall cease,
   And pass away at some sweet time of peace,
When naught but heaven doth all my thoughts
      engage?

Will many mourn me when I pass away
   From this frail, fleeting world? Or will but few
   Mix their sad tear-drops in the evening dew
That hangs in graveyards at the close of day?

But there are thoughts more 'wildering still than
      these,
   And fears almost too venturous to express,
   And longings over which the bitterness
Of darkness rolls like overwhelming seas!

Is there indeed a world beyond the grave,
   Where man shall live in endless bliss or woe?
   Or will he ne'er returning being know—
But fade like raindrops falling in the wave?

Is there indeed a God who reigns supreme,
   Somewhere far off in undiscovered space,
   Who sways the sceptre o'er the human race?
Or is He but a fiction or a dream?

O God! to think that I could ever doubt
   Thy being—Thee from whom all good doth run;
   Who art the bright and ever-shining Sun,
Which makes our dim lives glow like Thine.
   Without

Thee we would be like some poor helmless barque
   Tossing about upon a troubled sea,
   With none to point where sheltering havens be,
And none to guide us through the unknown dark!

Without Thee we could never draw a breath;
   Without Thee we could never move a limb;
   Without Thee our poor lives were dark and dim,
And we would pine and languish after death!

Throughout all Nature's wonders we can trace
   The unseen workings of Thy mighty mind:
   There's not a wild-flower opening to the wind
In which we cannot see Thy glorious face.

The daisy blushing on its native lea,
   The foaming cataract gushing down the steep,
   The prattling brook, the wild and wailing deep,
The sighing breeze—all speak to us of Thee.

Thy great Eye looked along the dreary vast
   Of space, ere yet the glorious stars were made ;
   Creation has Thy mighty power displayed :
The future lies before *Thee* as the past !

The universe is with Thy wonders rife ;
   From Thee come all our hopes and joys and
      fears ;
   Thine Eye alone can see the coming years.
'Tis well we do not know our future life !

' 'Tis better as it is ;' it may not be ;
   We cannot yet possess the great untold :
   As well believe the shallow brook would hold
The unfathomed mysteries of the boundless sea.

Our hearts could not contain it, did we know—
   All energy would cease, all hopes of fame ;
   All youthful visions of a glorious name
Would wing away, nor tell us where they go.

And bright-eyed Hope would, frowning, take her
    flight,
  And no more gild the future with her beam ;
  And Death would haunt us like a waking dream,
And every day would be as dark as night.

O Thou great Being ! far away, yet near,
  Thou ever-present, universal Whole,
  The living Element of every soul,
Dispel the shades and make the darkness clear ;

Forgive me when I wander from the right,
  Forgive me when I stumble in the gloom,
  Be near me on my pathway to the tomb,
And guide me to Thy everlasting Light.

THE NIGHT COMETH.

THE daylight waning and the darkness near :
  So little done, and still so much to do !
Before me the long night of cloud and fear,
  Without one star to pierce its shadows through.

I hear the rumble of the swaggering wains ;
  I hear the burden of the harvest song ;
And, through the hazy light in happy lanes,
  I see the sun-browned reapers pass along.

And I must lay my sickle down and go
  From the dim fields that look so drear and
      lone :
Alas ! that I have so few sheaves to show !
  I shall not hear the Master say, ' Well done.'

With what regret I look back to the past,
  When the long shadows loomed so far away,
And Morning seemed, on every wakening blast,
  To waft the whispers of an endless day !

So many misspent moments, wasted hours,
  Playing with pebbles on the sea - washed
    strand,—
Searching for butterflies or gathering flowers,
  Instead of toiling in the harvest land.

And now the Night stol'n on me like a thief,
  While yet I dreamt that it was scarcely noon,—
Sad that the sunshine is so very brief!
  Sad that the shadows fall so very soon!

Oh for one other hour of God's bright day
  In which to work with sinew, heart and will,
Ere yet I leave the fields and pass away
  To that mysterious sleep where all is still!

In vain, in vain! no answer to my calls,
  When from the gloom my spirit cries for light!
The last faint lingering gleam is gone, and falls
  Across the land the chill and starless night!

THE GUIDING STAR.

Sailing o'er life's uncertain sea,
  By counter-currents driven and tossed ;
No light to point where havens be ;
  My track amid the darkness lost :
The toil-drops trembling on my brow ;
  The shadows thickening everywhere ;—
Jesus of Nazareth, be Thou
  A Star to guide the wanderer !

When tempests wrack my lonely bark,
  And timbers strain, and sails are rent,
And billows howl, and heaven is dark,
  And cries are vain, and strength is spent :
Death grappling at my plunging prow—
  Destruction moaning in the air ;—
Jesus of Nazareth, be Thou
  A Star to guide the wanderer !

DREAMS.

In dreams we live a strange and mystic life,—
  We know not what is false and what is real:
Truth and untruth meet in perpetual strife,
  And all things are ideal.

A something-nothing state of nothingness,
  Where facts and fancies whirl in wild confusion;
Where sober life flaunts a fantastic dress
  Of mystical illusion;

And yet in dreams we think we move and live,
  All things seem actual and ordered duly:
What surety can our waking moments give
  That *then* we live more truely?

I have a fancy that life's fitful gleam,
  Where hopes are baffled and where hearts are
      breaking,
Is nothing but an unsubstantial dream,
  And death will be the waking!

LOVE'S DESPAIR.

FULL of the fever of a hopeless love,
　My heart's wild worship still is all thine own :
Unchanged—unchangeable—though doomed to
　　　move
　O'er life's dim waste alone.

Ah ! all too deep for words of mortal breath,
　My lonely love is one perpetual smart ;
Fain would I woo the quiet sleep of death
　For this unquiet heart !

'Tis death to see thee in thy joyousness—
　To meet thine eye, the smile upon thy lips,
And feel this world a blighted wilderness,
　And life a vast eclipse !

So sad and weary ! I would ask no more
　Than on thy breast to breathe my latest sigh ;
Like some worn wave that seeks a peaceful shore,
　On which to break and die.

ON THE SHORE.

I STOOD on the shore while the sad twilight drew
  Its gray veil across the blue heaven ;
And the deep-thoughted stars all looked holily
    through
  The vast bending vault of the even :
And numberless fancies came crowding o'er me
As I gazed on the desolate sea.

I thought of the long sunny days of my youth,
  When I dwelt by the murmuring billow ;
Of the yellow-ribbed sands and the pebbles so
    smooth,
  Of the beck that crept down by the willow :
And dreams of my childhood were borne unto me
In the dimple and dash of the sea.

I thought of a flow'ret that bloomed for the sky,
  A joy that was nipped in the blossom :
The eloquent glow of a love-lighted eye ;
  The heave of a fluttering bosom :
And the dirge of a lost love came sounding to me
In the murmur and moan of the sea.

I thought of a ship sailing into the west;
  Of hearts on her dewy decks grieving;
Of the tear - burdened eyelid — the quivering
      breast—
  The sigh for the land they are leaving:
And a passionate farewell was wafted to me
In the ripple and rush of the sea.

I thought of wild moments of ruin and wrath;
  Of mad billows boiling and seething;
Of a proud vessel swept from the tempest's dread
      path,
  Of a low wind above her grave breathing:
And some of Death's secrets were whispered to
      me
In the howling and hush of the sea.

I thought of the peace of a heavenly shore;
  Of a land where no broad sea can sever;
Of a glad light which sorrow can darken no more;
  Of a rest to the weary for ever:
And a chorus of angels seemed breathed unto me
In the tremor and thrill of the sea.

MY NEST.

THE shadows lengthen ; the twilight is falling :
  The labours and cares of the day are ended :
A peace settles over the city's brawling,
  Like the mirrored glow of the sunset splendid.
And sparrow and robin and skylark and throstle
  Are silent now in leafy recesses,—
Calmly and warmly and safely they nestle
  In the shadowy bliss of soft caresses.

On the skirts of the city *my* nest is waiting,
  Warm with a glow that is grateful and tender ;
And the world, with its striving and sinning and
      hating,
  Melts in the light of its sacred splendour.
What though my dovecot be poor and lowly ?
  Love's kingly sway makes the dwelling royal !
Peace, like a cherubim pure and holy,
  Fills every heart with a faith-life loyal !

Cosy warm nest ! every bounty and blessing
  Linger about thee as years o'er thee gather ;
Joys bide within thee, and mercies unceasing
  Rain from the bountiful hand of the Father !
Hope's budding promises break without number
  Rich 'mong thy leaflets, and burst into blossom :
Sweet be thy glad waking hours, and thy slumber
  Calm as the sleep of a babe on the bosom !

'On the skirts of the city *my* nest is waiting,
  Warm with a glow that is grateful and tender ;
And the world, with its striving and sinning and hating,
  Melts in the light of its sacred splendour.'

AT DEATH'S DOOR.

And so the fitful dream is almost over,
And no to-morrow will arise for me!
My spirit ebbs with the low lapsing sun,
And ere the last faint streak of lustrous gray
Is swallowed up of shadow, life must fail,
And darkness shall be my inheritance.
So be it: I can calmly welcome now
The slow up-creeping of the solemn waves
That come to wash me from the bank of Time.

Yet I have wept and murmured at my doom.
It is so sad to fall in the mid race
And watch my fellows all go sweeping by
To win the laurels that I dreamed might wreathe
In cooling circlet round my feverish brow:
A vain ambition, yet the sweetener
Of many a hard day's heavy-thoughted toil.

Ah me! the hours have perished when my heart
Throbbed thick to the still music of its joy;

And my strong soul, rejoicing in its strength,
Stood on the golden threshold of the morn
And heard the morning breezes whisper low
The promises of a long prosperous day.
I longed to flood the universe with song.
To song I gave myself, even as a maid
Yields all her being up to him she loves.
Nature stored all her riches in my heart,
To spring in flowers of song through aftertime.
The woods had secrets for my special ears,
The waves a melody none else could learn.
The dawn crept through me like a life renewed,
The painted clouds of sunset bore my soul
To spheres untrodden by the foot of man,
And in the lonely night the stars looked down
With wondrous revelations in their gaze.
Now all is over, and I pass away,
My cherished dreams of glory unfulfilled,
The splendours that I longed to weave unwoven,
And my great purposes gulped like a wreck
Whose scattered fragments, cast upon the shore,
But serve to hint of all the wealth that lies
Down in the silence of the ocean deeps.

Yet might I, like the swan, whose death-hour finds
The mid heart of all music, pour my soul
In one wild gush of intense melody,

So that throughout all time to come the world
Might hang in breathless worship on the echo
Of my last words, then it were sweet to die.

O Poesy! my mother, lover, friend,
My hope, my joy, my treasure and my god!
Could I but raise one little shrine to thee
On which might rest a shadow of the light
That dwells within thy deep and holy eyes,
Then gladly would I draw around my frame
The inky cloak of death, and take my way
To the cold region where Corruption sits
And darkness finds an everlasting home.

In vain, in vain! Yet wherefore should I weep
To leave this shadowy region's dusky marge
When brighter prospects beckon me away?
For there are other, higher worlds than this,
In which our quenchless lives at length may reach
Perfection's tireless manhood, in a sphere
Where failure never waits on fearless work,
But all the song that strove for utterance here,
And all the thoughts whose travail brought no
      birth,
Linked to the sweetness of a purer air,
Wed to the language of a nobler tongue,
Rich with a beauty past all mortal dreams,

May, breaking from the heart, bathe every star,
And be the music of Eternity !

Behold the sun has bid the land good-night,
And mortals hail him in another world.
Like him, my setting hour has come, and soon
Immortal dwellers on a far-off shore
Will give me greeting to their airy home.—
I hear the murmur of ten thousand seas,
I see the glimmer of angelic wings,
I feel a slumb'rous peace,—Can this be death ?

THE END.

Elliot Stock, Paternoster Row, London.

OPINIONS OF THE PRESS

On previous Editions of William Leighton's Poems.

———◦◆◦———

Westminster Review.

'The late William Leighton came of a poetical family. We remember being struck some years ago with the remarkable powers of description shown in Mr. Robert Leighton's poems. The nephew possesses much the same power and facility. A love for Nature in her quietest moods, and a vein of delicate fancy, distinguish the present poems. What Mr. William or Mr. Robert Leighton might have accomplished had their lives been spared it is impossible to say. We can but lament the early deaths of two relatives who were certainly endowed with poetical gifts of no common order.'

Edinburgh Daily Review (edited by Mr. HENRY KINGSLEY).

'The author of these exquisite poems was born in Dundee in 1841, and died at the early age of twenty-eight. Viewed as written by one so young, they are wonderful productions. They evince throughout a poetic genius of a very high order, and all breathe a fine, gentle spirit and a warm, tender, affectionate heart. They are full of thought and feeling, and are distinguished by felicity of imagery, great beauty of sentiment, and smoothness of versification. They abound with proofs of a passionate love of nature, and of a heart alive to sympathies and affections of friendship ; and along with these there is a wholesome manliness of tone, a high view of life and duty, which impart a healthful influence to the entire volume. We cordially commend the poems as productions of rare and varied merit, the effusions of a truly gifted and poetic mind.'

REV. GEORGE GILFILLAN, in Dundee Advertiser.

'They breathe a very genuine poetic spirit. Mr. Leighton, like all true poets, threw his heart into his verses, and there is scarcely a line in all this volume but seems transcribed from that unseen and red-leaved tablet, on which had been first written by the pen of the Almighty Himself so much that was fair, and good, and true, and noble. His poetry is simply and solely the effusion of his own fine and true-hearted nature, as it comes in contact with the lovely objects of the universe, or as it is touched to fine issues by his own feelings and passions . . . . They breathe a pure, a meek, and a holy spirit, resembling that of a noble and gifted woman like Mrs. Hemans.'

Sword and Trowel Magazine (edited by REV. C. H. SPURGEON).

'Softly sweet poesy, from one who now sleeps with his fathers. We were in years gone by favoured with verses from the pen which now indites no more good matters. From the grave this gracious poet sings.'

New Monthly Magazine (edited by Mr. W. HARRISON AINSWORTH).

'Throughout the volume all is simply beautiful, serenely and tranquillizingly agreeable, full of holy breathings and a rational piety, with excellent and faithful delineations, not of natural objects alone, but of the inner mind.'

Baptist Magazine.

'In the pantheon of the British poets he will rank with Kirke White, alike for the sweetness of his minstrelsy and the prematureness of his removal.'

Baptist Messenger.

'Sweet, precious, and refreshing.'

Churchman's Shilling Magazine.

'Sweetness, tenderness, and strength, together with a passionate love of nature, are the special characteristics of his verse.'

Church of England Magazine.

'We have much pleasure in recommending these poems.'

Dublin University Magazine.

'Mr. Leighton undoubtedly possessed a true poetic spirit. He evidently felt deeply and thought purely. His poetry displays great fertility of fancy and felicity of expression. To descriptive power of a high order he united a command of harmonious versification, while an ardent love of nature, and a manly, healthful tenderness of feeling, are the most pleasing characteristics of his muse.'

Family Treasury.

'Gems, all pure and sparkling.'

General Baptist Magazine.

'A tender and soothing influence breathes through these songs of the heart. They are sweet and healing as the balmy breezes of a sunny morning in spring. Marked by beauty, force, and feeling, they give strong evidence of a spirit that was filled with true poetic fire.'

Mothers' Treasury.

'These poems are all good, some of them exquisitely beautiful, and full of tender pathos.'

Treasury of Literature.

'Charming poems.'

United Service Magazine.

'A strong religious feeling is ever present, and the noble and manly thoughts are expressed in language that has the ring of true poetry.'

Young Englishwoman.

'Poems by a young man of real genius, "who died too soon for friendship, not for fame," William Leighton, a member of a poetic family, who gave a rare promise of eminence in literature.'

Athenæum.

'Good taste, sensitive feeling, and easy versification are their chief characteristics . . . The outcome of a generous meditative mind.'

Bell's Life.

'The versification is never at fault, and a certain natural refinement displays itself on every page. . . . The death of so promising a young man is in every way a calamity.'

Bookseller.

'A collection of exquisitely beautiful poems.'

 Opinions of the Press.

City Press.

' A sweet singer.'

Civil Service Gazette.

' It is a matter of great regret that the poet was not longer spared among us ; for that he was possessed of poetical power of a high and rare order is unquestionable, and has been acknowledged on all sides.'

Court Circular.

' Very beautiful verse, both pictorial and didactic.'

Era.

' There is scarcely a poem in the volume which does not give evidences of sincere thought and deep feeling, whilst there is a sweet and tender pathos in the majority which must command the attention.'

Freeman.

' The thought is generally of a high order, and there are many passages of exquisite tenderness and beauty. His strain is chiefly lyrical, and in that line he excels.' (' Baby died to-day' here quoted.) ' Many pieces as natural and tender will be found in the volume, which we heartily commend to all who are won by poetry which unveils the personal thoughts and feelings of the writer.'

Fun.

' Have the right ring about them. They are thoughtful and sympathetic ; and here and there among them are passages of much beauty.'

Graphic.

' Scotland may well be proud to claim amongst her tuneful sons the pure-minded, sweet singer whom she cannot but regret. . . . Had he lived, he must have won a high place in our literature ; as it is, he has enriched English poetry with many admirable pieces, which will live and set readers thinking for many a long day to come.'

Guardian.

' Tender and graceful poems.'

Iron.

' Obviously gifted with a fine nature, abounding in the domestic and social affections, and religious in the highest sense, he combined with these a delicate literary taste, and a true vein of poetic feeling.'

Judy.

' Ought to find many admirers. Pathetic and melancholy are many of the pieces, and through all breathes the true spirit of poetry.'

Literary World.

' All of them are good, and many are exquisitely beautiful.'

Lloyd's Weekly London News (edited by Mr. BLANCHARD JERROLD).

' William Leighton's music is of a nature that must have endeared him to all who came within the spell of his personal influence. The aspirations are noble ; the sentiments are chivalrous ; the fervour is manly.'

London Figaro.

' Exquisite productions.'

Methodist.

' We earnestly recommend these poems to all our readers. There is not so much to chasten and elevate our thoughts in daily life that we can afford to be indifferent to these ministers of purity and grace. . . . And remembering what William Leighton was, and how, through the laboratory of his mind, his experiences passed—some into the poetic possessions he has left us, others into the intangible essence which was constantly refining his nature—let those who live amidst the cares of business and money-getting, as he did, make companions of these perfect utterances, and strive, if not for their poetry, still for the purity which is the breath of them all.'

Nonconformist.

' William Leighton was a true singer, and on such themes as " Baby died to-day " was always simple, musical, touching. " Summers long ago" and " Rose" are very beautiful, and have a rare delicacy of finish.'

Once a Week.

'The tone of all the poems in the collection is thoughtful and earnest, and some of them breathe a spirit of deep and pure religious devotion.'

Queen.

'The natural expressions of a pure and tender heart.'

Reynold's Newspaper.

'Charming poetry.'

Spectator.

'The same qualities of tenderness, and grace, and melodious versification are to be observed throughout.'

Sunday Times.

'Gentle and devotional thoughts are breathed in language of much grace and refinement, and under all there is a vein of true and humanizing pathos.'

Sunday School Times.

'Full of tenderness, sympathy, and genuine Christian feeling.'

Weekly Budget.

'The only words to express our opinion of these charming poems are those of unqualified commendation. They disarm criticism ; for when we would examine rigorously, their sweet tones enter into the heart, exciting its deepest sympathies, and winning us to admiration.'

Weekly Dispatch.

'Displays both refined feeling and culture.'

Morning Post.

'Whoever loves sweetness and vigour, thought and feeling, will admire and love the charming poems of the late William Leighton. May the daisies be plentiful on his too early grave !'

Evening Standard.

'Charming and tender pages.'

Aberdeen Journal.

' They are sweet and pleasant.'

Bath Express.

' They are natural, vigorous, and sweet, and polished with the touch of a scholar's hand.'

Beverley Recorder.

' Sweet and pure and beautiful are the sentiments they express.'

Bolton Weekly Guardian.

' " Baby died to-day " and " Our lost one " have the simple beauty and pathos of some of Wordsworth's.'

Boston Guardian.

' The entire collection breathes the spirit of genuine poetry.'

Bradford Observer.

' The poems show a genuine poetic power, many of them being full of a tender, refined sweetness, and a music all their own.'

Brecon County Times.

' Our apology for dwelling so long on this small book of poems is— their general excellence, their sweetness, their pathos, and truthfulness to life.'

Brighton Gazette.

' Amongst the selections of verse which will be handed down to posterity as the most charming productions of the present age are the few included in the small work of the most admired pieces of the late William Leighton.'

Cardiff Times.

' Breathe a genuine poetic spirit, and seem the effusion of a noble, true-hearted, and withal pious, nature.'

Clare Freeman.

' They are no unfit companions for the works of our higher singers, who graced the annals of our literature.'

Clifton Chronicle.

' For tenderness and grace these poems are hardly surpassed.'

Derby Mercury.

' Distinguished by elegance of diction, graceful versification, tender, rather melancholy, tinge of thought, strong religious feeling, and a passionate love of the beautiful in nature.'

Derbyshire Courier.

'Tenderness, delicacy, sweetness and affection, characterize his verses, and here and there we find outbursts of melancholy reminding us of Kirke White.'

Dewsbury Chronicle.

' Throughout they are remarkable poems.'

Dover Express.

' Beautiful in imagery and sentiment, the lays are tinged with a shade of melancholy which reminds us of Henry Kirke White's poetry.'

Dublin Morning Mail.

' The world would be better if we had more of poetry like his—breathing a deeply religious spirit, united with an ardent love of nature, much descriptive power, and sweetly modulated verse.'

Dumfries Courier.

' Sweetly flowing verses.'

Dumfries Herald and Register.

' Mr. Leighton was evidently a warm-hearted man of genius.'

Dundee Courier and Argus.

' He was a member of a gifted family, Mr. Robert Leighton, a poet of a high order of genius, who, before his death, had attained a widespread reputation as an original and gorgeous word-painter, being his uncle. . . . The poetic remains of William Leighton were written in the intervals of business, yet one of the characteristics of his writings is their high artistic finish, suggestive of scholarly retirement rather than the harassing cares of commercial and city life. Gifted with a true poetic instinct, which sympathized with Nature in all her moods, his writings abound in bright pictures of some of Nature's aspects, which must appeal to the most prosaic souls. . . . The book, taken as a whole, well deserves perusal. It is, in fact, one of those pure wayside wells whose deep clear waters and green, flower-gemmed margin refresh the traveller in the dull and parched highways of life.'

Exeter Flying Post.

' Their beauty and tenderness, and sweet poetic melody, should secure for their gifted author a lasting name.'

Forres, Elgin and Nairn Gazette.

' All these pieces breathe an exquisite sweetness.'

Glasgow Herald.

'There is much to admire all through. All of the poems are more or less tinged with earnest feeling, and convey their meaning in language of true and exquisite tenderness.'

Glasgow News.

' Will be cherished in the memories of all who can sufficiently appreciate his clear and sweet productions.'

Greenwich and Deptford Chronicle.

' A very wealth of the most pure imaginings—the sweet, tuneful utterances of a gentle, all-sympathetic, poetic nature ; vibrating with delicate soul-touching harmony here, there stirring with strong, occasionally sad, emotional force, everywhere persuading us that the strains are those of a true poet. There are three descriptions of rare and beautiful verse (if we may venture to divide it thus) in the book : the personal or domestic, the sacred or Scriptural, and those devoted to what might be termed strictly natural themes, a graceful lyrical power being common to each.'

Halifax Guardian.

' Excellent lyrical poetry, full of feeling and tenderness.'

Hampshire Telegraph.

' Some of the poems are unspeakably tender and sad, and all of them betoken a pure and delicate fancy.'

Haverfordwest and Milford Haven Telegraph.

' These exquisite little gems have the true ring of poetical genius in almost every verse.'

Hawick Advertiser.

' They are not mere rhymes, but genuine poetry, abounding with beautiful imagery, delicately expressed.'

Hawick Express.

' It contains many poems of exquisite pathos, and a deep religious sentiment pervades the whole.'

Huntly Express.

' He has written some poems which the world will not willingly let die.'

Isle of Wight Advertiser.

' Charming word-painting.'

Isle of Wight Chronicle.

' Veritable gems of word-painting, welling up from a pure, sympathetic, and deeply impressible heart.'

John o' Groat Journal.

' The work is full of tenderness, religious thought, and exquisite poetical feeling.'

Kelso Courier.

' In William Leighton we had a man of genius, whose lofty conceptions and melodious muse became loftier and sweeter as they soared away above the trivial things of time, and expressed in pathetic verse the anticipations and hopes of a glorious eternity.'

Leith Burghs Pilot.

' Those who carefully read these poems cannot but be profited and made to feel the seriousness of the theme, as well as the tenderness and power of the singer.'

Lincoln Gazette.

' Exhibits unusual genius, sweetness and vigour, and is full of thought and feeling.'

Liverpool Weekly Albion.

'Their sweetness will win them appreciation.'

Liverpool Courier.

'A poet of whom Liverpool has reason to be proud.'

Liverpool Porcupine.

'A legacy of poetry, instinct with tenderness and sweetness, and lovely with the perfect loveliness of truth and purity. . . . We must send our readers to the book itself. We promise them a pleasure and a surprise—pleasure in the tender sweetness and simple beauty of the poems it contains ; and surprise that such poetry should have been written by a young man whose occupations were so antagonistic to the cultivation of the imagination.'

Londonderry Sentinel.

'The poems of a gifted young Scotchman, whose noble, sweet, and pathetic poesy, clothed in the tenderest beauty, purity and sublime imagery, display the genuine ring of heaven-born genius.'

Lynn Journal.

'It is to be deplored that so gifted a word-artist should have been cut off so early in a career which foreshadowed the highest hopes.'

Manchester Examiner and Times.

'The poems are marked by an absence of pretence, and by a tone of dignified humility. . . . The author was evidently a man of deep sympathetic feeling, and of no ordinary culture.'

Manx Sun.

'A pleasing collection of poems by this young and gifted poet.'

Market Harborough Advertiser.

'Grace, purity, refined feeling, and great felicity of diction are characteristics of all his poetry.'

Middlesborough Daily Gazette.

'Brimful of genuine outbursts of poetic genius.'

Newbury Weekly News.

'The author was undoubtedly a true poet.'

Northampton Herald.

' A rich legacy of poetic sweetness and beauty, which will keep the memory of the writer green in thousands of hearts for many a year.'

North Devon Herald.

' Every line he wrote was instinct with an all-pervading piety, and a fine and ardent love of the beautiful. There is the true ring in his verses —they are the outpourings of a sweet and sympathetic nature, which, even from the midst of uncongenial and antagonistic surroundings, was able to pour forth its sorrows, its joys, its hopes, its fears, in exquisite and melodious lays.'

Nottinghamshire Guardian.

' They are full of thought and tenderness, and are remarkable not less for beauty and grace of versification than for refined feeling and culture.'

Oldham Chronicle.

' We consider him to be a genuine poet—tender, true, pure.'

Oxford Times.

' Will be welcome to all lovers of true poetry. The simple little poems breathe a sweetness and beauty not often found in this age of straining after effect ; they are evidently the outpourings of a gentle and poetic mind.'

Oxford Undergraduates' Journal.

' It is seldom indeed that a reviewer has the genuine pleasure of noticing such poems as these . . . This thin volume abounds in true poetry, full of high and noble thoughts, expressed in sweet and charming verse. The gifted author was an enthusiastic lover of Nature, and delighted to dwell upon her mysteries, and describe her beauties. Exquisite tenderness, great beauty of imagery, and graceful versification are combined with a vigorous, manly tone, and a simple pathos which would have raised Mr. Leighton, had he lived, to a very high place among English poets.'

Oxford Weekly Messenger.

' Ought to find its way into every house in England.'

Peterborough Standard.

' It is with real pleasure we have read the poems, and it is with much sincerity we would commend them.'

Peterhead Sentinel.

' We will introduce the reader to two or three of his poems—conceptions of beauty and full of tenderness—which will live for ever.'

Portsmouth Times.

' Had he lived but another decade, William Leighton would, in all probability, have ranked with the noblest and truest poets of modern times.'

Prescot Reporter.

' Every page contains something highly pleasing.'

Scarborough Mercury.

' More touching and exquisite poetic compositions than those contained in this little book we have never met with.'

Sheffield Independent.

' Tenderness, delicacy, sweetness, and affection characterize his verses, and here and there we find outbursts of melancholy reminding us of Kirke White.'

Shrewsbury Chronicle.

' His early death undoubtedly deprived the world of much of that description of poetry which it does the world good to read and to be delighted with.'

Southport and Birkdale News.

' The death of so lovely a disposition, and the extinction of powers so needed to make fragrant the dusky path of less gifted men's lives, is a loss of no common magnitude.'

Sunderland Times.

' We are satisfied that the author possessed not only true poetic genius, but that he had the faculty of clothing his thoughts in that beautiful and pure language which alone is capable of expressing the finer sentiments of human passion and feeling.'

Sussex Daily News, Brighton.

These are the poetic remains of a gifted soul, possessing value of remembrance, of life-work, and soul-love.　We recall "The Leaf of Woodruff" upon its first appearance in one of the magazines, when people mused over the authorship of the touching poem, which was quoted far and wide.'

Tunbridge Wells Gazette.

' All bear the impress of a true poet.'

Western Daily Mercury.

' Evince throughout a poetic genius of a very high order, and breathe a fine, gentle spirit, and a warm, tender, affectionate heart.'

Yarmouth Gazette.

' Poetry remarkable for sweetness, and distinguished by tender and sympathetic feeling.'